M. A Bird, Mary Bird

The Hawkshawes

A Novel. Vol. 2

M. A Bird, Mary Bird

The Hawkshawes
A Novel. Vol. 2

ISBN/EAN: 9783337273491

Printed in Europe, USA, Canada, Australia, Japan

Cover: Foto ©Andreas Hilbeck / pixelio.de

More available books at **www.hansebooks.com**

THE HAWKSHAWES

𝔄 𝔑𝔬𝔟𝔢𝔩

BY

M. A. BIRD

AUTHOR OF "SPELL-BOUND," "THE FATE OF THORSGHYLL,"
ETC. ETC. ETC

IN TWO VOLUMES

VOL. II

LONDON
JOHN MAXWELL AND COMPANY
122, FLEET STREET
MDCCCLXV

CONTENTS

OF

THE SECOND VOLUME.

———

THE HAWKSHAWES

CHAPTER I.

REGINALD AIDS IN THE FULFILMENT OF THE PROPHECY.

" I WILL tell you the rest in as few words as I can," continued the young man, after a pause. " After I had seen my brothers, my greatest wish was to speak to them, and make friends with them. I know now that they would have scorned the friendship of a gipsy boy, and laughed, had he claimed kindred with them; but I thought of nothing at the time except the pleasure of making myself known to them, and telling them that they should each have an equal share of the property after their father's death. I did not know that they had been murdered a

few days after I saw them, but my mother
did, and told me of it afterwards. They
were poisoned by their grandmother, because they did not resemble the Hawkshawe
family! and she wished the property to pass
to a distant branch who were Hawkshawes!
Can you wonder that I hate that old woman?
Can you wonder that in my savage, un-
tamed state I should desire to kill her?"

"Oh, Reginald! If you had killed her!"
said Ellen, shuddering.

"I do not think it would have burthened
my conscience very heavily," he replied;
"but I now rejoice that I did not harm her,
having no ambition for the office of execu-
tioner. I reproach myself far more for
that chance shot," he added, mournfully.
"though Heaven knows I would sooner it
had gone into my own breast! 'Tis well
that I have not killed Lady Clarissa, though
I fear she will do more harm before she
dies; however, that is merely a conjecture

—a vague fear, and does not concern *your* precious life. I was wandering about in the neighbourhood of the house, hoping, as I told you, to see my brothers, when I encountered my father. I knew him by sight, and did not avoid him. He seemed struck by my appearance, and asked me my name, which I would not tell him. He asked me to go with him, to which I readily agreed, as I thought I should then surely see my brothers. The woman who had nursed me was sent for, and several old servants, who had lived in the house when I was born. They all said that I was certainly the lost heir of the Hawkshawes; and when they saw this mark, with the name tattooed beside it," and as he spoke, he showed Ellen his arm, just above the wrist, "they were all ready to swear to my identity. You have heard somewhat of my ungovernable temper, and you have, unfortunately, seen somewhat of it too; but the accounts have fallen very short of the reality. I was more like a demon than a human being. However, I need scarcely tell you that. You know, too, how your gentle influence has roused the good, and subdued the bad that is in me. And now, sweet Ellen, I have told you the whole story of my life, up to the present moment. If the future be brighter and better, it is to you that I shall owe it. No doctors of divinity could have lectured me, or goaded me into submission; but your gentle wooing ways, your pretty airs of authority that seemed to say I *must* obey you, because you were so beautiful; your sermons and grave reprimands, which it would have been unmanly not to listen to with deference— all this, and above all, a suspicion that my father, until he himself conceived a passion for you, would not have hesitated to sacrifice you, body and soul, to my advancement, threw around you a halo of divinity

that made me respect, while I passionately
loved you; and made me a tolerably tract-
able pupil, by impressing on me the deference due from a gentleman to a lady. You
look surprised, Ellen ; you did not guess at
all this. Yet I have not deceived you.
You were mistaken; and that I did not set
you right is the only deception I have prac-
tised on you."

He paused, and stood looking over the
sparkling sea, with a calm, melancholy air.
Ellen watched him with a sort of awe.
Then he looked up to the bright blue sky.
From the shelf of rock where they stood
little was visible but sea and sky, the top
of the cascade where the water made its
first spring over the rock, and by leaning
forward, the strip of beach below, with its
edge of foam, and the lonely cairn that
marked the gipsy's grave.

Ellen watched the expression of his noble
face, but would not interrupt, by one word,

the current of his thoughts. She recalled the impression left by his countenance when she first beheld it; there was the same regularity of feature which had struck her then, only improved by the thick curly beard, and paler and thinner from the effects of close application to study; but yet how changed the face was! She had watched the alteration going on from day to day, or it would have been difficult to believe that the calm, dignified, intellectual man before her, was the same being as the wild, half idiotic-looking youth whose appearance had so startled her on her first introduction to him.

"When I go," said Reginald, at length, in a low, sad tone, "it is possible that we may never meet again. Even if we do, it may only be for a very brief period; and our next parting will, in all probability, be for ever. This will not be from my own wish or choice, sweet Ellen; you will not suppose anything so absurd as that; but I mean, simply, that such may be my fate. You do not love me, Ellen; but you feel some interest in me, particularly as regards my 'eternal welfare,' as you call it, and I should not like you to be made miserable by the thought that I died an atheist, supposing it possible that such a being can exist out of Bedlam. I will not say that I believe all you have tried to teach me, but I should not fear to yield up my soul to my Maker, whenever it is required, satisfied that a just God will not punish an imperfect creature, because his acts and thoughts partake of the imperfection with which he was born." .

"Even this limited belief is something to rejoice at, compared with the awful darkness of your former state," said Ellen. "You do, then, firmly believe in the existence of a God?"

"How can I look abroad upon this fair

earth, upon the sea, the sky, the sun, the stars, and feel a moment's doubt?" he exclaimed. "How can I become acquainted with any fact in Nature, from the vast orbit of a comet, to the structure of the smallest insect's wing, and think that all this came by chance! Why, *chance* might have placed a monkey's head upon that pretty neck of thine, or terminated those delicate fingers with the talons of a cat! No, no, Ellen; I am no believer in chance. Could chance give the faculty to write a good book? Could chance give man that wonderful power of thinking, and expressing his thoughts in language? But I must talk no more, for the sun is low, and I have yet to show you the track down the cliff, and the place where the boat lies. I will leave with you my copy of Carlyle's works, and then you can judge for yourself whether I could possibly read and relish that man's writings, and be that mixture of imbecility

and wickedness which must go to the composition of an atheist. Now give me your
hand. Step firmly; keep your eyes steady,
and there is no danger."

He led her down a difficult and zigzag
path, and they stood together on the beach,
midway between the cairn and the mouth
of the brook. The cascade fell about a
hundred yards beyond the cairn. Where
the brook formed a small estuary, there
were several large masses of rock which
appeared to have fallen from the cliffs
above at some distant period. Two of
these formed a creek, where a small boat
was lying, secured by a chain to an iron
ring fixed into the rock.

"She is high and dry now," observed
Reginald, "for the tide is at the ebb. At
the flood she floats, and it is then easy to
guide her into the current, which will carry
you out into the bay. See!—this is the
way to cast her loose. Now mark this,

Ellen—if the brook is very full, and comes rushing and foaming down more than it does now, you must on no account attempt to put out to sea. By heavens! I think I must be mad to show you this way at all. I feel like the Ancient Mariner, compelled by some internal force to speak out. But reason assures me that you are not likely to make use of my information; and I dare say the supernatural prompting is merely the desire—not very supernatural nor surprising either—to gratify the whims of my darling little friend."

Ellen did not speak, for some of Mrs. Hawkshawe's dying words, which had completely escaped her memory amid the agitating scenes that followed her death, were now ringing in her ears. "He shows her the way of escape!" This was all she could recall, though she strove hard to remember the rest, feeling convinced that the words were prophetic.

"What are you dreaming of?" asked

Reginald, tenderly. " Are you sailing in imagination over the moonlit sea, with a soft summer breeze bearing the boat gently along?"

" No," she replied, " I was not thinking of that ; though I fully believe I shall have to go out on this sea, moonlit and clear, or dark and stormy, as it may happen to be."

" I fully believe the contrary," said Reginald, " or I would not leave you. However, to make your mind more easy, be assured that everything shall be done to facilitate your escape. A rope shall be fixed up along the pathway, and a life-belt shall be placed in the boat, which I particularly beg of you to put on before starting. And now we will talk no more about this insane project."

" There is one thing you have forgotten," said Ellen. " Which way am I to go?"

" Round that headland," he replied. " Give it a wide berth—that is, keep at a

good distance from it, and you will easily
double it. On the other side lies a fishing-
village, where you can get help. And now
let us go back. We shall be missed."

The ascent of the rocky path was less difficult than the descent. When they reached
the hermitage, Reginald again pulled off
his boots, which he had resumed before
their descent to the beach, and carried
Ellen safely through the streamlet to the
dry turf of the garden. While her companion re-adjusted his *chaussure* she wandered out upon the lawn, where she was
somewhat surprised, and little gratified to
find Mr. Hawkshawe, who very seldom
honoured the garden with his presence.

Ellen had more than one reason for dis-
liking this man; for besides his unprin-
cipled conduct with regard to her letters, he
had assumed a tone of gallantry towards
herself which was highly disagreeable. She
could not account for the antipathy she felt

for him. It was violent and instinctive.
It was not allied to fear, it was not indigna-
tion at his baseness, though she shuddered
when he approached her, and felt her lip
curl and her nostrils quiver when he addressed to her words of covert admiration.
There was some element in her repugnance
beyond all this, which she could only define
by saying that she disliked him *because* she
disliked him. When she now saw • him
advancing towards her, her first impulse
was to run away; but this feeling was
instantly checked as worse than useless, and
she only slackened her pace to a still slower
saunter, that she might not go beyond
Reginald's hearing.

"All alone, Miss Maynard!" said Mr.
Hawkshawe, in an insinuating tone. "Wandering 'in maiden meditation, fancy-free,'
to enjoy the congenial loveliness of this
exquisite evening? Or are your dreams
devoted to some one thrice happy mortal,
who——"

"I was thinking, sir," interrupted Ellen, with as composed and business-like an air as she could assume, "that, as your object is now accomplished, and your son is thoroughly awakened not only to the necessity of study, but to an ardent love for it, you can very well dispense with my services."

"I think I have somewhere a written document," said he, in a slow, determined tone; "dated the twenty-third of last September, and purporting to be a solemn pledge and promise that you would remain in my family for a full year. It is now June, Miss Maynard."

"But, sir, the object for which I came being accomplished——"

"We will not talk of the object, but of the promise," said Mr. Hawkshawe, drawing closer to her side. "I cannot consent to part with you, sweet Ellen. Wait yet a little while, and you will see what fate and fortune may have in store for you."

She felt his hand touch her waist, lightly indeed, but it startled her like a galvanic shock. At one spring she cleared the little brook by which they were standing, and stood on the other side, wrathfully facing her enemy.

"Reginald is within call, Mr. Hawkshawe," said Ellen. "Do not make me the cause of another altercation between you."

"Nay, nay, Miss Maynard, you are too hasty," said Mr. Hawkshawe, with a slight laugh. "I would not for the world offer you the least insult, though I confess that my feelings of gratitude and almost paternal affection led me to be too familiar in the expression of them. For this and all my other offences against you I offer an humble apology; and do not suppose that I mean to force you to remain here against your will after Reginald is gone. His wish is, as I suppose you are aware, to enter the army, and go to the Crimea."

"Go to the Crimea!" repeated Ellen, turning deadly pale; "he did not. tell me that!"

Mr. Hawkshawe's cheek also blanched, and his black eyes glared as he watched these signs of emotion; but he quickly recovered himself, and went on in an unmoved tone.

"Yes," said he; "and he will shortly go to town to effect the purchase of a commission, and make all the necessary arrangements. This is his present intention, but we cannot always calculate upon the permanence of a young man's whims; and he *may* return home, or have to wait some months for his commission. When that business is settled, when I am sure that he will not need your teaching any longer, your present engagement shall terminate, and you shall be free to depart, although there may yet remain some months of the period for which you agreed to stay."

"That is all that I desire or expect, sir," said Ellen.

"Then we may consider that question disposed of," said Mr. Hawkshawe. "Reginald will not be gone more than a week at farthest, and I hope you will be able to pass away that time with your books and music, though you will be left in solitude."

"Are you going to accompany your son?" asked Ellen, hastily.

"I think not," he replied, looking rather black at the hope that was implied by the vivacity of her question, "but I shall probably have to go to Plymouth on business."

Ellen inclined her head in reply, not being able at the moment to frame a sentence that should not appear too much like a desire for his absence. Reginald at that moment emerged from the shrubbery, and Mr. Hawkshawe soon after took his departure.

About a week after the visit to the hermitage, Reginald presented to his tutor
(who was only a curate with a small stipend)
a comfortable living in the north, which
was in his father's gift, observing afterwards to Ellen, that it was an easy way of
getting rid of the old gentleman without
paining his feelings.   But Ellen had seen
the glow of delight that accompanied the
gift, and she knew that it was from gratitude and regard for a worthy man, and
from no selfish impulse, that he had impor-
tuned his father for the presentation to
this living on the death of the former incumbent.

In another fortnight Dr. Gibson and his
sister were gone, and the carriage stood at
the door waiting to convey Reginald to the
railway station.   He had bidden adieu to
Ellen in the library.   Lips had quivered
and hands had trembled as they took a
formal and ceremonious leave of each other,

and he was half-way across the hall when he ran back to give her one parting injunction. She was sitting on a sofa with a book in her hand, just where he had left her.

"Ellen," said he, as he approached her hastily, "if you *should* have to use the path through the hermitage (though I do not think you will), don't forget to take a towel with you to dry your feet, or you may take a severe cold. And should you really resolve to go, burn a light in one of your bedroom windows all night, and you will find trusty friends in the hermitage in the morning. I will give orders that your windows shall be watched. The friends may be rough-looking fellows, but you need not fear to trust them. They will take you to a place of safety, or obey any orders you may choose to give them."

"Thank you, Reginald," said Ellen, without raising her head.

2—2

"What! not one smile!—not one farewell glance!" said he, stooping to look into her face. "Tears, Ellen!—dear Ellen! are those shed for me?"

"You know I love you as a brother, Reginald."

"As a brother!—ay, true," he repeated, sadly. "Yes, yes — very true — as a brother!—only as a brother! Then as a brother let me kiss away my sister's tears."

He kissed the drops from her eyes and cheeks, pressed her hand, and was gone. A foreboding shiver passed through her frame, for she felt that that parting "might be for years, or it might be for ever."

CHAPTER II.

THE DOVE IS IN DANGER OF FALLING A PREY TO THE HAWK.

THE day of Reginald's departure was to Ellen a long and gloomy one, which she tried to ascribe to the weather, which was chill and rainy.

She could not eat—she could not read; and when she sat down to the piano, it chanced by some fatality that every piece she played recalled vividly some scene in which those same harmonies had been instrumental in soothing Reginald's turbulent moods, or rewarding him for application to distasteful study.

It was very odd, she thought, that the

absence of her usual occupation should
make her feel so dull; and she furtively
wiped away her "quiet" tears, and ignored
their existence.

Women, and perhaps men too, often
cheat themselves most egregiously with
regard to their own sentiments. Any impartial observer, taking into consideration
all the circumstances, would have decided
that Ellen grieved over Reginald's absence,
and was depressed by the vague dread
which possessed her that that absence
might be indefinitely prolonged. But
Ellen would in no wise admit this. If the
imaginary impartial observer had been in
actual bodily presence, and had assured
her, with that ostentatious candour which
persons of that kind are fond of displaying,
that her tears flowed for Reginald—that
her whole thoughts were of Reginald—
that her sighs were heaved for Reginald
—that her fears were alarmed by the

dangers he would meet at the seat of war
—that her heart beat proudly when she
thought of the noble daring that prompted
him to rush into honourable danger—had
this unpleasant observer taken a mental
photograph of her inmost soul, and laid it
before her, she would, with perfect good
faith, have denied the accuracy of the
picture.

Perhaps the still small voice of conscience
was going through some process of this
sort, for, as the twilight shadows were
closing around her, she suddenly started
up with an air of consternation, and took
from her desk a miniature portrait of Frank
Willoughby. Did she confess to herself
that this was the first time during the
course of that day that she had recollected
his existence? Probably not; for by one
of those subtle courses of self-deception
which women practise on themselves, she
began to attribute all her sorrow to her

separation from Frank, and all her anxiety to the dangers to which he was exposed.

She stood in the recess of a window, contemplating the picture. It represented a handsome manly young fellow, in regimentals. The countenance was open, good-humoured, and genial, but a physiognomist would have noticed a want of decision and firmness about the mouth. Ellen looked intently, and presently a change came over the face she looked upon. Strong, straight, black eye-brows took the place of Frank's light, delicately arched, and pencilled ones. The laughing blue eyes became dark and steady, burning with a smothered fire. The fine Grecian nose expanded into larger and bolder outlines; the brow became higher and broader, and black masses of hair swept over it like raven's wings; while the lower part of the face was clothed in a short but majestic beard. In fact, her imagination had covered poor Frank's picture with the lineaments of Reginald Hawkshawe.

She had heard no step, no noise of opening or closing door, but a sudden shiver warned her that Mr. Hawkshawe was behind her. She looked round with an air of haughty inquiry into the cause of his intrusion.

"There must be a strong sympathy between us, Miss Maynard," said he. "You were so absorbed that I am sure you did not *hear* me."

"It is a sort of mesmeric attraction or repulsion," said she, with a slight emphasis on the last word. "I feel it towards some persons."

"I trust it is not repulsion in my case," said Mr. Hawkshawe; "but at all events there was a strong counter-attraction in the portrait. Is that your *fiancé*?"

He took the picture from her hand, for she was too much frightened to withhold it, and examined it closely in the lingering daylight.

"This is not the man whom Nature intended to be your husband, Ellen," he said. "This face expresses a vacillating character which could not long command your respect."

"It also expresses candour and nobility," said Ellen, thinking of the letters, but refraining from more pointed allusion to them, for fear of rousing further enmity between Reginald and his father.

"Both very estimable qualities," returned Mr. Hawkshawe. "But do you suppose that your heart will crave nothing more in your husband? If you think so, let me undeceive you; let me tell you what you *will* require—what you *will have*—what you *must have*. A loftier intellect, a character of more firmness and energy than this delicate youth's; above all, a passionate, all-absorbing love, such as a young coxcomb like that could never feel!"

And he cast the picture from him in disdain.

Without stopping to pick it up, Ellen rushed towards the door, but she was detained midway by the strong hand of her pursuer.

"Stay—stay," said he, "it is useless to run away. You *must* hear me. The love that can alone come up to the exalted ideal of your fond young heart must be the love of a man whose soul has been tried and purified in the fire of suffering; not that of a youth whose admiration would be divided between you and his looking-glass. You must be *my* wife, Ellen!"

"You dare to say this," cried Ellen, indignantly, "and your wife still living!"

"I know that I have the appearance of a wife," he replied, calmly—"a ghastly phantom, that sits at my board like the skeleton at an Egyptian feast. But she will be no impediment long, dear Ellen.

Her disease has taken a fatal turn, and she cannot live many days."

"Then wait at least till she is in her grave before you talk of another marriage," said Ellen, hoping to gain time by temporising. "And why are you here at all, Mr. Hawkshawe? Did you not promise me solitude during your son's absence?"

"Stratagems are allowable in love and war, you know, fair lady," he replied, with a laugh. "I merely said that to lull you into security."

"Then you uttered a deliberate falsehood!" said Ellen.

"You cannot make me angry with you, dearest," returned Mr. Hawkshawe. "And now the stratagem having succeeded, and placed you absolutely in my power, you must surrender to my terms."

"Never!" exclaimed Ellen, firmly.

"Hear first what they are," said he— "simply that you shall give me a written promise to become my wife within three days after my present wife's death."

" Detestable monster!" exclaimed Ellen. " Such a proposal does not need denial."

" You refuse me, then?" said he.

" Absolutely," she replied. " With scorn. contempt, and hatred, do I refuse you."

" Be it so!" he said; and he frowned till his black brows met. " You have signed your own doom. I would have wooed you gently, Ellen, as fair lady should be wooed. I would have been your slave; for when a man of my age loves, he gives no divided affection."

" Sir!" cried Ellen, struggling to free her arm from his grasp, " must I repeat that it is an insult for you to speak to me of love?"

" Not so, dear one!" he said, attempting to fold her in his arms, but only succeeded in possessing himself of her other hand; " in extraordinary circumstances, extraordinary proceedings are allowable. You must not look upon me as a married man. Consider how many years my unhappy wife has been a miserable idiot."

"What made her so?" asked Ellen, hoping that, if there were any truth in the housekeeper's story, this question would rouse his anger, which she would much prefer to his love.

"Grief," he replied, in a low, stern tone—"grief for the loss of her children." His back was towards the window, and she could not see how pale he had become.

"And with that piteous spectacle daily before your eyes, constantly recalling the terrible cause of her misfortunes, you can be so unmanly as to speculate upon her death, and address proposals of marriage to another woman?" said Ellen. "Mr. Hawkshawe, this is not love! It is some monstrous and selfish feeling that a demon would be ashamed to own!"

"Go on," he said, in an admiring tone. "You·look so infernally handsome when you are angry, that I could almost wish you were a confirmed shrew! Socrates might well adore his beautiful Xantippe, if she were only half so lovely as you are! With that blushing, indignant, averted face—those flashing, resentful eyes—the eloquent lip and nostril, quivering with anger now, but showing in their sensitive movements how ready the thunder-storm is to end in a passionate rain of tears—with all this you look so enchanting in your present mood, that I can hardly believe it possible for me to love you more when you are gentle, tender, and dove-like, as I will teach you to become."

"You will see me in no mood but my present one, Mr. Hawkshawe," she replied, striving to suppress the symptoms which had excited his admiration; "for, believe me, were you even free to marry, I could never become your wife. Though you are restrained by no feeling of decency, this assurance ought to satisfy you. Let go my hands, sir."

"Not," he said, raising her right hand to his lips, "until this little prisoner has signed the articles of capitulation."

"I would cut it off sooner!" said Ellen, indignantly.

"Then I fear you will compel me to make you a prisoner altogether," said he.

"You dare not! I defy you to do it!" cried Ellen, with an appearance of unshaken courage, though her heart quailed within her.

"There are few things that I *dare* not do," replied Mr. Hawkshawe, "and locking you up is certainly not one of them. You do not like the idea of being a prisoner; I can see that easily, though you carry it off with a firm and resolute air. Give me your promise to marry me three days after my wife's death, and I will set you free. You would not break your word."

"And therefore I will not pledge it to what I cannot and will not accomplish," said Ellen.

"Tut—tut," he ejaculated, contemptuously. "You must not talk in that childish way. Be reasonable, Ellen. Understand that you *must be my wife*. Dost thou comprehend me, child? There is no choice offered thee, except to take thy fate kindly, or reduce me to use coercion."

"And where then are the laws of my country, and my rights as an Englishwoman?" she demanded.

"The laws are doubtless quite safe in the statute-book," he replied, with a laugh that made her blood curdle; "and as for your rights—they are all very well in theory, like everything else, until opposed by practice. When you are mine, Ellen, I will defend your rights! but just at present I

am sorry that you compel me to make them
bow to my might."

Ellen took a brief and rapid mental
survey of the position in which she was
placed.

"If I am a prisoner," she said, "let me
at least be alone. Quit the room, sir, and
if you are so fond of the office of jailer,
lock the door."

"No, my charmer, this room is not to be
your prison," said he. "You express so
much willingness to be locked up here, that
I suspect some means of escape. No—no.
Not here! You must remain in your bed-
chamber."

He endeavoured to lead her from the
room, but she made such a vigorous resistance that he was obliged to carry her. She
shrieked for help, but all in vain. He had
closed the doors leading to the hall as he
came along, and her screams could not be
heard. He carried her upstairs to her own

bed-room, put her in, and taking the key on the outside, quietly informed her that he was going to lock her in.

" I do not care for that if I am free from your presence," she retorted, angrily.

" There is yet time for you to change your mind and listen to reason," he said, ere he closed the door. "I warn you, Ellen, that you will repent of your obstinacy. Even yet you may sign that promise."

" I will not!" she answered, resolutely.

" Then be the consequences on your own head!" he replied. " To-morrow you will be glad to do it. Think well over my words. There may be one more chance for you."

He withdrew, locking the door after him. Immediately the bolts inside were drawn, and some heavy piece of furniture was placed against the door.

" Barricade the door as you will," he

whispered through the key-hole; " you are locked in, but *I am not locked out!*"

His step was heard retreating down the long passage, and she stood fixed to the spot, frozen by the horrible thoughts suggested by that fiendish whisper.

" Not locked out!" she repeated, peering round the gloomy chamber, and dreading to see the lofty figure of her persecutor emerge from the obscurity. " Oh, Reginald, Reginald, why did you abandon me! But I must not waste time in vain regrets; what short space I have must be given to action. *Not locked out!*—how can that be? Ah!— the secret door by which Mrs. Hawkshawe entered! But where is it? How shall I discover it? I have no light. Stay—here is a box of matches—that is something."

With a trembling hand she lighted one of the matches, and by its feeble and short-lived ray examined the wall near the head of the bed, where she knew the door must

be, as it was on that side Mrs. Hawkshawe
had appeared. Her very anxiety and trepi-
dation retarded the accomplishment of her
wishes. Her hand shook, and the matches
went out, or she struck them so violently
that they broke off instead of igniting.

"This will not do!" she murmured. "I
never needed nerve and presence of mind
so much, and all my faculties seem to be
deserting me. Merciful Father, aid and
protect me! and deliver me as a bird from
the snare of the fowler!"

With more composed feelings she renewed her search, and as the last match but
one was consumed, she discovered that one
of the panels slid back into the wall, leaving
just space for her to pass through.

The last glimmer of light showed her
that this opening did not lead immediately
into the large apartment in which Mrs.
Hawkshawe died, but into what looked like
a closet or passage. That she should have

light to discover the means of exit from this place was of the utmost importance, and having but one match left, she reflected how to supply the deficiency. It did not take long to decide. Having screwed up several long rolls of paper, she put a quantity more into the fire-grate, and then with a steady hand lighted the sole remaining match.

CHAPTER III.

THE ESCAPE.

TRIFLES become important by the circumstances under which they occur. Ten thousand housemaids daily strike lucifer matches into light, and at the slightest distraction—the quarrelling of two dogs in the street, or the sound of a hurdy-gurdy—will stand a-gape till it is burnt out, and then deliberately light another. " It is only a match." But of what quite infinite value was that one little match to poor Ellen! More than life depended on its burning or not burning. She scarcely dared to breathe, and dreaded lest her hand should start involuntarily and extinguish it. All is well!

It burns—the paper in the grate is lighted, and she is so far towards safety.

As she threw a shawl around her she thought of Reginald's parting injunction. It is so pleasant to obey the wishes of those who love us. She rolled a towel round her arm that she might not drop it in her flight, and then lighting one of her paper torches, proceeded to the secret passage. With the aid of her eyes it was easy to undo the fastenings on the opposite door, but she would have found it impossible to do it in the dark, and her grateful thanks rose to Heaven in a joyful murmur. Having set both panels open, she returned and extinguished her torch, for the moon shone in fitful glimpses, and would suffice to light her on the well-known way to the library, and the fastenings of the window leading into the garden were so well known to her, that she could undo them in the dark if she found them secured.

The night was wild and stormy, and she thought with terror of the boisterous sea on which she was to put forth; but she dreaded the sea less than the wicked man into whose power she would inevitably fall if she remained, and so she went on, unhesitating. She regretted much that the want of a lamp or candle prevented her summoning Reginald's rough gipsy friends to her assistance. How gladly, she reflected, would she now have hailed one of those swart faces which had so terrified her on the night of Mrs. Hawkshawe's funeral! But she placed her trust in a higher than mortal power, and gave but a passing and momentary regret to the precarious helps of earth.

After passing through the secret doors she re-closed them carefully, and stood in the gloomy chamber where the wild and unhappy spirit of the gipsy had forsaken its tenement of clay. She was not superstitious, but a chill ran through her veins as she recalled the circumstances attending the last time that she had stood within that apartment. In addition, she had the discomfort of not knowing in which direction to find the door, as the moon was at that moment overclouded, and then for the first time the question arose in her mind "whether the door would be unlocked." Cold drops of terror stood upon her brow, and her eyes seemed to protrude from their sockets in their endeavour to penetrate the darkness. At that moment a bright gleam of moonlight streamed through the window, and she found herself face to face with the deceased Mrs. Hawkshawe. It was as much owing to the paralysis of fear as to self-command that she suppressed a shriek that might have led to fatal results; and the moon fortunately shone sufficiently long to show her the mistake she had made. It was not Mrs. Hawkshawe's spirit, but her portrait, before which she stood.

Ellen felt greatly relieved, and impelled by the urgency of flight she made no pause, but darted to the door. Alas! it was locked —and the key gone! She looked round in despair, and by the last glimmer of the again overclouded moon she caught sight of another door, opposite to that by which she had entered, and apparently leading to another room of the suite. She found it —groped for the handle, and with unspeakable joy discovered that it was not fastened. A very faint light from the windows showed her that she was in another large and lofty room. There was a door on the side towards the corridor, but that was locked; cheered by former success, however, she sought for and found the means of egress into another apartment of the suite.

The wind was now howling fearfully, and the rain at times descended in torrents. She could hear the brook raging in its rocky bed, and she remembered Reginald's warn-

ing on no account to put off in the boat if
its waters were higher than usual. An idea
struck her:—instead of exposing herself to
almost certain death alone on the raging
sea in that stormy night, she would seek
refuge with Mrs. Sweetman. The good old
lady would conceal her during the night,
and aid her to escape in the morning.

With increased spirit, and a much
lightened heart, she continued her endeavours to get out of the long suite of rooms
in which she found herself. The outer
door of the next room was locked on the
inside, but the key remained. By an exer-
tion of strength with which the urgency
of terror alone could have supplied her,
she turned it in the rusty lock. The door
came open with a loud cracking noise, and
she found herself in a passage; but whether
it were the one into which her own room
opened she could not distinguish. She
closed the door, as she had been careful to

do with all the others, so as to leave no traces of her flight, and stood for a moment pondering on the way she ought to take. The house clock struck eleven; but the sound reverberated so confusedly through the arched passages (remnants of monastic architecture) that it did not enable her to form a guess from its direction as to what part of the building she was in.

As the echoes died away another sound struck her ears. It was a strain of mournful, wailing music, rising at last to what sounded like a shriek of agony, and then descending through the plaintive intervals of the minor key into a low sobbing, like the inarticulate utterance of one that has no hope.

"That Eolian harp again!" thought Ellen; and yet she trembled with an undefined feeling of dread, and without further delay hurried down the passage, away from the side whence those mysterious sounds proceeded.

Tall, narrow windows lighted this passage on one side; and on the other was a row of low, arched doors, probably belonging to the dormitories of the monks. Again the music sounded, and now nearer than before.

Something beat and flapped against a window within a few feet of her. It was no doubt a white owl; but to her bewildered imagination, it looked strangely like a pale female face, with the long hair streaming wildly on the blast of the storm.

Ellen staggered on a few steps further. Her limbs trembled so violently that she could scarcely stand, and a deadly faintness was creeping over her. She made a desperate effort to retain her senses, and had just, by one failing glance, ascertained that she was near the end of the passage, without any outlet except into the monks' cells, when she beheld a sight that instantly restored all her strength and energy.

Just entering the passage behind her, and thus cutting off all retreat, was Mr. Hawkshawe, carrying a light in one hand, and supporting with the other the tottering steps of the decrepit beldame, Lady Clarissa.

Ellen tried the nearest door: it resisted her frantic efforts to open it. Like a wild bird fluttering in a paroxysm of fear against its cage, she threw herself against the next —the last! It yielded, and she entered, but wished she could retreat again, for it bore evident signs of being the very spot towards which her enemies were bound. There was a fire of charcoal in the grate, and a large table in the centre covered with chemical apparatus. To attempt a retreat would, however, have been only to throw herself into the remorseless grasp of her deadly foe.

There was no alternative but to conceal herself in the cell, and await a chance of escaping. The means of hiding were fortu-

nately soon found. A table, crowded with
lumber, stood in one corner, yet not so close
but that it left space enough behind it to
admit of Ellen's crouching there, with little
risk of discovery. She was hardly settled,
and was still offering up a voiceless prayer
for protection in her great danger, when the
door was opened.

" Why did you leave the door unlocked?"
demanded the old woman, in a shrill queru-
lous tone.

" There was no danger in leaving it for
so short a time," replied her son. " Do you
imagine that any one of the servants would
venture here after dusk, especially with the
Wail sounding so loud, to say nothing of
their dread of the Grey Maiden looking in
at the windows."

" You saw something as we came along,"
said the hag, seating herself slowly in a
chair that was placed at the table; " I felt
you start and tremble. What was it?"

" A white owl, I believe, beating against the window," he replied. " There is a nest of them in the old clock turret just above."

" It was no owl," said Lady Clarissa, in a sepulchral tone. " It was the Grey Maiden herself, depend upon it. *I* have seen her. I saw her the night your father died, and I looked at her till I could have drawn her picture. Take care that you do not give another Grey Maiden as an heir-loom to your family."

" There's no fear of that," returned Mr. Hawkshawe. " Marriage will make all right in a day or two. I would not be so hasty, but that I must have this business settled before that headstrong boy returns."

" Ay—ay," said the old woman. " And it is said that your ancestor meant to make all right by a marriage, when he wronged the Grey Maiden, and shut her up for the night in a dark cell. But in the morning he found her dying, with her brown hair turned grey; and she cursed him with her last breath, and promised to haunt him and all his descendants on their death-beds. That promise has never been known to fail."

"I have no fear," replied her son. "Ellen will neither die nor curse me. I will teach her to bless, and love, and live for me."

"Teach her what you like, I care not," said Lady Clarissa, with a laugh of derision. "I shall be well pleased to see her pride humbled. Come—let us go to work."

While she spoke the Wail swept up the passage, and seemed to pause at the door and utter its loudest shriek. Mr. Hawkshawe glanced round uneasily.

"Do you hear that?" asked his mother, raising her withered yellow hand. "Her doom is fixed! The Wail rises loud at the mere mention of the work we have in hand."

"I wish it would not sound so loud,"

said he; "it seems loud enough for two deaths. I never heard it like that before."

"I have," said Lady Clarissa, gloomily. "Come, hand me that crucible."

They proceeded for some time in their operations, which Ellen watched with intense interest, having a vague idea of the object they had in view. "Are you sure you recollect the recipe exactly?" asked Mr. Hawkshawe, with some anxiety, as the old woman paused, as if undecided.

"I recollect it well," she replied; "I was but dwelling on the time when I first learnt the secret. I was young and beautiful then, Reginald."

"Will you not impart the secret to me?" he asked.

"No," she replied, "it is an accursed knowledge, and brings no happiness on its possessor. Thou art better without it, my son."

" Will this draught be ready for use to-morrow?" he inquired, after a long silence, during which they had assiduously continued their operations. "The obstacle to my marriage must be removed as speedily as it can be done with safety."

" She may have it to-morrow at breakfast," said the old woman; "and in ten minutes you will be free to lead Ellen Maynard to the altar."

" I would that I had yielded to your wish, and given her *this* dose on that dreadful night when she saw, or thought she saw, the spectres of her children," said Mr. Hawkshawe, gloomily. " It would have been a crime the less to answer for; and it is horrible to have destroyed her mind!"

" Will moaning over it restore her mind?" said Lady Clarissa, snappishly, "or if you are so penitent, would it not be more reasonable to let your wife live, and leave your pretty Ellen for your son to marry? I'll answer for it, she would prefer him to you."

"No!—curses on him and——,"

It sounded almost as though this imprecation included his mother, but hateful as she was, Ellen distrusted her ears.

"We must have some more charcoal," said Lady Clarissa, chuckling, as she always did when she had succeeded in rousing her son's anger. "Have you got any here?"

"I must fetch some," he replied, moodily. "but I must take the lamp; you can do with the fire-light while I am gone."

He took the lamp and a basket for the charcoal, and departed.

Now was the moment for Ellen's escape. If she awaited Mr. Hawkshawe's return she must infallibly be either discovered, or locked up in that horrible cell to perish of hunger. Better than that the wide sea, with heaven's free air and sky!

The old hag was cowering over the fire, mechanically warming her hands, and occasionally picking up bits of charcoal, and placing them round her crucible.

Ellen crept out from her hiding-place. She would willingly have overset the table and destroyed the ingredients of the hellish mixture, but she had gathered from their discourse that the chief of these was in the crucible, and any such attempt would have ruined her own chance of freedom, without preventing the accomplishment of their plot. The instinct of self-preservation was irresistible. The door had been left ajar, the old woman was deaf, and did not hear the rustle of her dress. She passed quickly across the room, and found herself in the comparative freedom of the passage, just as Mr. Hawkshawe's light was disappearing at the other end.

The death music might wail, and the grey spectre flutter against the windows now; Ellen heeded them not. There were worse spirits still dwelling in mortal bodies than any that gibbered and flitted in less substantial guise.

Her light step roused no echo as she fled along the oaken floor. When she gained the corner she saw Mr. Hawkshawe descending a flight of stairs. She followed, and found that there was another passage beyond the stair head. Along this she sped, rapidly as might be, and presently reached the large central staircase. Now she knew her ground. But her terror was so great that she had now no thought of anything but escaping completely from the house. In two minutes she stood breathless within the library. With eager, trembling hands she undid the fastenings of one window.

She is free! She is in the garden, with the wind blowing, and the rain beating, but she is free! Across in all haste to the hermitage. It is a mere ceremony to take off her boots and stockings, they are so wet already; yet she takes them off, thinking

of Reginald. Following his directions she
wades through the water, and smiles sadly
as she thinks of his parting injunction
about the towel. When her boots are on
again, she spreads the towel on the little
altar.

"He will never see me again," she thinks
with a sigh, "but this will show him that
I thought of him to the last."

Then she took a knife from her pocket,
cut off a long curl from her hair, laid it
upon the cloth with a stone upon it, lest
the birds should take it to line their nests,
and dashing away some blinding tears,
went her way to the boat.

The rope was securely fixed, and well
was it for her that it was so, for the violence of the gale threatened at almost every
minute to blow her off the narrow path.
She did not dare to return to the hermitage,
for Mr. Hawkshawe would be sure to discover that she had got out by the library

window; he might even trace her footsteps
on the moist turf, and no corner of the
garden would be left unsearched. He
might find her there, and that possibility
was more appalling than the fiercest tem-
pest.

She reached the boat. Even in its shel-
tered nook it was bumping about against
the rocks; but she thought not of that. It
was afloat, and that was sufficient.

Again she bethought her of Reginald's
instructions. The life-belt was there, tied
to the seat of the boat. It could scarcely
be of any use, she thought, in such a night,
but she inflated it, and buckled it round
her waist.

It seemed in this utter extremity, when
she stood, as she thought, face to face with
death, that her soul threw off the garment
of hypocrisy that it had worn for her
own deceiving, and gave itself up without
reserve and without shame to the passion

that monopolised her heart. She did not say to herself that she loved Reginald, but she thought of him, and only him; and that with a tenderness and devotion that would have astonished her, had she had time to reflect upon it. Only once she remembered Frank Willoughby, and then with a sigh she murmured, "Poor Frank! he will grieve for my death! But he will soon forget me!"

The prospect of being, in a short time, separated for ever from Reginald choked her with grief, not for her own fate, but for the anguish he would feel; and if she prayed for life, it was more for his sake than her own.

In a lull of the storm she cast loose the boat, and put out upon the rushing current that poured in floods through the narrow gulley. She gave one vigorous push against the rock to get as far as possible towards the centre of the stream, and then laid

down the oar, and seized the rudder. Fortunately the boat did not capsize, which
was more than she had dared to hope for.
She kept the helm steady, and in a few
moments was out at sea, tossing like a cork
upon the eddying waters.

Obeying Reginald's instructions to steer
wide of the headland, and perfectly aware
that however terrible the open sea might
appear, her only chance of safety lay in
keeping clear of the land, she kept her
eyes upon the tall cliff, and carried along
by the ebb tide, stood out towards the
middle of the bay. While she looked, the
rock assumed a reddish tinge. It deepened
to a lurid glare, and the dancing waves, as
they rose, caught the same hue upon their
crests. She turned her head—Gracious
Heavens! the Priory was in flames!
Then Mrs. Hawkshawe's words burst upon
her—"See how the flames arise! The
guilty ones are consumed! The boat—

the boat! it will be dashed to pieces! No
—it is safe upon the sands, and she is
rescued!" She felt a deadly torpor steal-
ing over her senses. With a last effort she
slid from the seat to the bottom of the
boat, that she might not fall overboard,
and consciousness forsook her. ·

CHAPTER IV.

CRIME BRINGS ITS OWN PUNISHMENT.

When Mr. Hawkshawe returned with a fresh supply of fuel, he found Lady Clarissa cowering over the fire, just as he had left her, looking like—

> The foul witch Sycorax, who with age and envy
> Was grown into a hoop.

She raised her head when the light from his lamp fell upon her, and returned, with her bleared and filmy eyes, the stern gaze which he fixed upon her.

"Is anything amiss?" she demanded, at length. "Have you met any more ghosts? This is a fine night for them."

"Ghosts!" he repeated, contemptuously, "not I! I was thinking of far different matters."

"There was one here a while ago," continued the old woman. "I saw it gliding past the door, like a tall black shadow; but it vanished before I could make out what it was like."

"Tush!" replied her son, "you indulge in such dreams till you think them realities."

"They are not always dreams," she said; "they are real enough sometimes to the sight, to the hearing, even to the touch."

"Do you forget how you once strove to make me believe the contrary"? he asked, in a stern voice.

"Yes, yes, I remember," said she, hurriedly, "but that *was* a dream—a mere delusion."

"I would I could feel sure of that," said Mr. Hawkshawe. with a groan.

" You felt sure then," she said, " why do you doubt now?"

" There is too much to encourage doubt," he replied, gloomily, " you encourage it yourself by always avoiding a direct answer to my question. You know to what question I allude. Will you not answer it now?"

" Ay," she said, drawing herself nearly upright in the chair, " I will answer it as I have ever done, by asking in return, how you dare to put such a question to your mother?"

With an impatient shrug, Mr. Hawkshawe pointed to the crucible, while he fixed a stern and searching glance upon Lady Clarissa, and his compressed lips quivered with the emotions that he would not suffer himself to utter.

" I see—I see," cried the hag, with a diabolical chuckle, " you think that if I can make this pleasant sleeping potion for one, I could have made it for another. Is that the only way you have of showing gratitude for my services? I had best break the crucible to atoms and suffer its contents to consume in the fire."

She raised the poker to carry her threat into execution; but her son arrested her hand.

"Nay, nay, you are too hasty," said he, "let the deed we have resolved on be accomplished. It is but half a murder."

"Do you suppose that God will judge you as an English jury would do," said the old woman, "and acquit you of the charge of murdering your wife because death was not inflicted at one merciful stroke? You destroyed her mind by one subtle poison, and now——"

"That was your act, not mine," interrupted Mr. Hawkshawe; "you feared she might disclose facts that would endanger your life; and yielding to your entreaties,

I consented to your giving her a drug which you said would suspend her mental faculties for a time. You have rendered her a hopeless idiot."

"And now you wish to complete the work, and remove her altogether," said his mother; "and that you call committing only half a murder! You are but a degenerate Hawkshawe if you cannot do courageously that which it is your will to do, and call the act by its right name too. You cannot, by giving it a milder name, make murder anything but murder. Your wife is in good bodily health, and likely to outlive you by many years. To-morrow morning you drop a little colourless liquid into her coffee, and in ten minutes she will be dead. If you were seen to do it, and any traces of poison could be discovered in her body, what pretty name do you think the coroner's jury would give to your performance?"

" You say there will be no traces of the poison left," said Mr. Hawkshawe, thoughtfully; " and none could be found in the bodies of my children."

" And what does that prove?" said Lady Clarissa.

" Only that poison *may* have been present," he replied, " though the chemical tests were wanting that would have detected it. Why do you still evade giving me satisfaction on this point? Can the worst reality be more injurious to you than the suspicions that constantly haunt my mind? I pledge you my word, as I have often done before, never to divulge the secret to anyone, even after your death."

" You are an ardent lover, upon my word!" cried the old woman, jeeringly. " Your fair bride awaits you, locked up in her chamber, and yet you waste time here in trying to extort a confession of murder from your mother! Leave the past alone.—

I and the past will go to the grave together."

"You *shall* tell me!" exclaimed Mr. Hawkshawe, grasping her arm. "Did you poison my children? Answer me! If you refuse I will lock you in this dismal den till you confess the crime, or clear yourself by an oath!"

"You think to conquer *me!*" cried Lady Clarissa, with a tone and glance of unutterable contempt. "Fool that you are! Who talks of conquering *now?*"

With her disengaged hand she had taken a small bottle from the table, removed the stopper, and as she uttered the last words she flung some of the contents in his face, drawing back, and averting her own, as she did so.

The effect was instantaneous. Violent convulsions shook his frame. But she had miscalculated upon one point. The gripe upon her arm involuntarily tightened. In

5—2

his struggles he fell upon the ground, dragging her after him. The table was overturned, and the lamp broken; but not, alas! extinguished.

The flame caught some papers over which the contents of a large bottle of spirits of wine had fallen, and the room was instantly filled with flame. The wretched pair saw the fate that was impending over them; but Mr. Hawkshawe, though perfectly conscious, was totally unable to control his own movements; and the miserable old woman had not strength to drag him a single inch towards the door, nor even to reach another bottle towards which she stretched her hand with frantic but impotent endeavours.

"Let go for one moment, Reginald!" she shrieked. "Let me reach the antidote! It will cure you in an instant! Let go! Let go!"

She tried to force his hand open, and

had partially succeeded, when it closed again like a vice, compressing one of her fingers in a grip of iron. Held now by both hands she was even more helpless than before.

Her struggles soon became terrific, and her yells filled the cell and the corridor; for a tongue of flame swept up her neck, and set fire to her hair and head-dress. Still her son lay extended on the floor, speechless, and now motionless, though his face expressed the tortures he was enduring, as his clothes became ignited, and slowly burnt upon him. Large drops poured from his brow, and his eyes were fixed upbraidingly upon his mother.

"I confess!" she shrieked—"I confess! I murdered them—I poisoned them! Now let me go! I confess! I confess!"

Her own evil deed was visited upon her. He had no power to let her go, nor himself to escape from danger. He could only look at her in dumb agony, as he held her in that convulsive clutch.

The horrid scene lasted but a few moments. The miserable woman's yells were for that brief space incessant. She writhed like an eel, and strove to tear away his hands with her toothless gums, and still the last object she beheld, before the fire had destroyed her sight, was his face distorted with agony, and his large distended eyes fixed on her in silent reproach. A moment afterwards her shrieks ceased suddenly—her head fell back, and her sufferings were over.

Yet shrieks and wailings might still have been heard, mingled sometimes with sobs and laughter, now outside the windows, now beneath the vaulted roofs of the antique corridors. A white object fluttered and flapped against the casements. Perhaps the owls were attracted by the sight of the flames. The superstitious would have believed that the avenging spirit of the race looked in with triumph on the destruction of her enemy's descendants.

Other cries soon began to sound through the house; the cries of human beings shouting the terrific word "Fire."

The servants were aroused, and the inhabitants of the neighbouring village were rapidly collecting. Had they been on the spot on the first alarm they would have been too late to save their unhappy master. As the lifeless and blackened body of his mother sank backwards, one deep, dreadful groan escaped him. Did a thought of Ellen cross his mind, locked in her chamber and perhaps doomed to the same horrible death that he was suffering?—Who can know?

Then the smoke gathered thicker around, and ended his torments.

Wider and higher spread the devouring flames; the entire wing of the Priory was speedily in a blaze that, seized by the storm blast, and whirled and wafted in wild sport, cast a lurid glow for miles around, tinging the peaks of rocks far away, and gleaming on a little boat with one poor frightened maiden in it, floating out at sea.

CHAPTER V.

REGINALD HEARS THE DEATH WAIL.   HIS
HASTY RECALL TO ST. OSYTH'S PRIORY.

On his arrival in London, Reginald betook
himself to the hotel recommended by his
father, and where his name was a guarantee
for every species of civility.   He dined, and
strolled about the crowded streets for an
hour or two, observing the novel scene with
dignified interest.

At length, having completely lost himself in the labyrinth of streets, he called a
cab, and directed the driver to go to the
—— Hotel.

He had so little the air of a raw country-

man, that the cabman never dreamt of
doing other than going straight to the spot,
where, accordingly, his fare was deposited in
less than two minutes. It was a sad mistake. If the poor fellow had known the
real state of the case, he might have made
a three mile circuit, and demanded a crown;
but in blissful ignorance he pocketed his
shilling, and vanished from the scene.

Reginald's slumbers that night were
feverish and disturbed. He dreamt that
he stood by his mother's deathbed, and
heard the prophetic words that she had
uttered. All came back as clearly as when
it actually occurred. He awoke in alarm.
The wind was high, and he thought of
Ellen. What if, in terror of his father, she
had persisted in trying to make her escape!
No, he would not believe it. Besides, had
he not secured against such risk by com-
manding the gipsies to watch her window?
Was it likely that on such a night of

all others she would attempt to go to sea alone?

This reflection comforted him. He arose and drank a glass of water, bathed his hot brow, and composed himself to sleep again. To sleep, but not to rest. The same dream haunted him, even more vividly than before. He awoke with a start. How the wind howled! It whistled through the keyhole, or some crevice, sounding like the cry of a woman in agony.

Good Heavens! It was the Death Wail of his family! He hid his shuddering face in the pillow. Mrs. Hawkshawe he had seen that morning in good bodily health.

"Is it for her?" he asked himself. "Merciful Heaven keep my father innocent of that crime! Better that it were for himself!"

But the wind sunk, and the Death Wail was no longer audible. The young man reasoned with himself, and came to the

conclusion that after all it had been only
the wind whistling through the keyhole,
and that his heated brain just wakening
from a fit of nightmare, had converted it
into the warning of death. He slept again
after some time, and now his sleep was
quiet and dreamless.

In the morning he had almost forgotten the
nocturnal disturbance; and when the early
post brought him a short letter from his
father, containing some trifling commission
which had been forgotten, he felt perfectly
easy. The letter concluded with these
words, which it may readily be imagined
were the cause of its being sent at all:
" Miss Maynard, I understand, has been
playing and singing all day, so I conclude
she does not find her solitude very irksome."

" He has not intruded upon her, then,"
was Reginald's very natural conclusion.
" That is all well. What a fool I was to be
so disturbed by a dream !"

After breakfast he presented himself at the Horse Guards, and was occupied till late in the afternoon in the business attending the purchase of a commission, which he expressly stipulated should be in the regiment to which he knew Ellen's lover belonged. The name of his favoured rival he intended to extort from her on his return home, which was the principal, if not the sole reason for his urging her to remain there during his preliminary visit to town. He would obtain the names of all the officers, and try the effect of each upon her tell-tale cheeks.

He returned to his hotel in high spirits. All was going well. The mortality had been great in the regiment of his choice, and he was assured of a speedy appointment.

" A person has been waiting nearly two hours to see you, sir," said a waiter. " He is a messenger from the Electric Telegraph Office."

The messenger stepped forward. During the previous night a great part of St. Osyth's Priory had been burnt to the ground, and Mr. Reginald Hawkshawe's presence was required immediately. The message was sent by Oliver Clark.

"When does the next train start?" demanded Reginald, in a hollow voice.

"In a quarter of an hour, sir," replied the waiter, "Bradshaw" in hand.

Reginald gave a sovereign to the messenger, sprang into a cab, and was off at full galop to catch the train. There was a little bustle and consultation and wondering at the hotel; then his rooms were locked, that nothing belonging to him might be disturbed, and the business of the establishment subsided (if such a word is applicable here) into its usual routine of hurry-skurry, for the landlord felt no anxiety about his bill.

Reginald did not utter a word on his

journey. Some other passengers got into the carriage, but at the next stage got out again, to find more lively company. He was enduring tortures of suspense, from which only time could free him.

"The wail was no fancy then! Pray heaven it may have been for Lady Clarissa! Something terrible must have occurred, or why should the message be sent by Oliver, and not by my father? And more than all —is Ellen safe?"

Such was the theme on which his anxious thoughts rang the changes, while he sat with folded arms and clenched teeth, as though wrought up to endure with fortitude the agony of some surgical operation.

The carriage was waiting for him at the station, but Oliver had returned to the Priory, leaving word for his young master that he had thought it best to do so, as there was no one there to give any directions, except Mrs. Sweetman, and she had been

so frightened she was like beside herself.

"Where is my father?" asked Reginald,
when the coachman had delivered this
message.

"Please, sir, you'd better not ask till you
get home," replied the man, crumpling his
hat in his hands nervously; "please, sir,
I'd rather not say nothing, because I mayn't
know just the rights of it."

"Answer me at once, blockhead!" exclaimed Reginald, shaking him by the collar.
"Where is my father?"

"Oh, sir, pray forgive me," said the poor
fellow, while the tears streamed down his
cheeks, attesting his sincerity, "I don't like
to tell you such bad news. Mr. Hawkshawe is dead, sir. His body was found
this morning, or I should say, yesterday
morning, among the ruins. And Lady
Clarissa's too, sir," he added briskly, as
though the latter part of his intelligence

were some counterpoise to the gloom of the former part.

"My father dead!" said Reginald, pressing his broad palm upon his forehead, "but why should you say there was no one to give directions? Where is Miss Maynard?"

"Oh, sir, she's burnt too, there's no doubt; for she can't be found anywhere."

"Has her body been found?" gasped Reginald.

"No, sir, but they were digging for her when I came away, and I dare say they've found her by this time."

"Drive like the devil!" was Reginald's concise order, as he sprang into the carriage.

The coachman obeyed as closely as he could without killing his horses, and almost before they stopped, reeking with sweat, at the Priory gate, their impatient master sprang out.

Oliver had heard the approaching wheels, and appeared at the door, looking paler, and more woebegone than ever.

"Is Miss Maynard found?" demanded Reginald.

"No, sir," said the old man, in some astonishment that the stranger should be mentioned before the members of the family, "we can't find a trace of her, but perhaps the body is consumed. Will you come this way a moment, sir," continued Oliver, leading his master out of earshot of the other servants, "there's something very unaccountable about Miss Maynard, sir."

"What is it?" exclaimed Reginald. "Tell me quickly."

"Why, sir, after the alarm and confusion about the fire was over, and the other two bodies had been discovered, which I suppose you know, sir, they *was* discovered?" said the old man suggestively, for his mind misgave him whether the coachman had said more than that Miss Maynard was missing.

"Yes—yes—I know," said his master, impatiently, "my father and Lady Clarissa —they are past help, Oliver; but my anxiety is for those who may yet be saved. What of Miss Maynard?"

"Well, sir, I thought it right to see if any one else was missing, and then we found that no one had seen Miss Maynard all the day. We went up to her room, but the door was locked, and we could make no one hear; so thinking she might have been frightened into a fit by the fire, we burst open the door. There was a chest of drawers leaning against it, inside, sir, and two bolts drawn, but the young lady was nowhere in the room, and besides that, she had not been to bed the night before, for it was not disturbed at all. When we had searched in closets and

6—2

presses, and everywhere, and the rest had all gone out, I caught sight of a small chink in the wainscot, so I looked, and found it was a sort of sliding door, sir, and it led into the room where the picture of your honour's mother is kept. There can't be a doubt but what Miss Maynard got out that way, sir; but where she is gone is more than I can guess."

"I will examine the room myself," said Reginald, and darted upstairs.

A short glance showed him that all was as Oliver had stated; the only additional fact being the quantity of burnt paper in the grate. On examination he also found traces of paper and matches about the secret door. This seemed strange. Why should she burn matches and paper if she had a candle?

He looked at the windows. No signs of lamp or candle there, yet the servants might have removed it when they searched the room. But again the blinds were down, and she would have drawn one up if she had placed the signal for the gipsies.

He returned to the door. The key was gone; and wherefore all this barricading? He was heart-sick with anxiety. Some wrong and violence there had been; but to what extent?

He dashed down stairs to the library. The shutters of one window were open, and there was her desk, unlocked, and on the ground a miniature portrait. He caught it up—it was that of a young officer, who he felt sure must be Ellen's lover.

"Poor fellow!" he said, as he thrust it into his breast pocket, "he has lost her, I fear!"

Perhaps he had; but whether that loss should be much subject for regret to Reginald remained to be proved.

He hastened across the garden, and

dashed through the water, boots and all, into the hermitage, in the hope that she would have remained there till the storm abated.

Vain hope! There was indeed the proof of her having been there, but she was gone. He looked at the towel, which showed that even in the terror of her flight she had recollected his injunctions, and another object caught his eye,—the lock of hair! With a shout of joy he seized upon the treasure, and called her name till the cavern echoed; but there was no reply.

Perhaps she was on the beach. Down the steep and slippery path he sped, giving a hurried glance below to see whether she had fallen down the precipice. No sign of her to be found, but the boat was gone! He leaned against a rock, the very picture of despair, and looked out upon the sea.

Hope is the most difficult of all feelings

to destroy, especially in a young heart; and even while he looked so utterly desponding, hope began to revive. The boat was a little tub-shaped thing, at which he had often laughed, and promised himself a better one; but she lay on the water like a duck, and was almost as difficult to overturn. As long as Ellen's fate was uncertain he could not bear to think that she was not alive.

Inspired by this new gleam of hope he sprang up the rocky path again, pausing now and then to cast a keen glance over the sea, to discover, perchance, a little boat tossing upon its waters. The waves were dancing under the slant rays of the morning's sun, but no dark spot was visible.

"What weather had you here on the night of the fire?" demanded Reginald, bursting into the kitchen, where the servants, including Mrs. Sweetman and Oliver, were assembled. The housekeeper was too nervous to remain in her own room, and Oliver had just been reading a chapter of the Bible to them.

"Dreadful stormy, sir," replied Oliver, "but fortunately it blew from the north-west, or every bit of the house must have been burnt."

"Would to God it had! so *she* had escaped!" muttered Reginald. "Saddle my horse," he added, aloud.

While the groom was gone to obey this order, Reginald suddenly recollected that he had neither eaten nor drunk for twenty-four hours. He cut a crust from a brown loaf that stood on the table, and told Oliver to fetch him a glass of wine. While the old man was pouring it out he ventured to ask his master if he would be pleased to give orders respecting the ——, here he hesitated, the bodies of his honour's father and grandmother.

"Oliver, my friend," said the young master of Hawkshawe, laying his hand kindly on the old servitor's shoulder, "I leave all to you. See that everything is done that should be done for the family credit. Of the family *honour* it were perhaps best not to speak. Till one point is cleared up, I cannot show respect even to my father's remains. See to it all."

"I will, sir," said Oliver. He shook his white head as he watched Reginald gallop off at full speed. There was something wrong, he saw, but what, he could not guess, excepting that it had reference in some way to Miss Maynard.

After a sharp ride of some fourteen miles Reginald drew bridle at the door of a village smithy. The grinning smith came out.

"Welcome to your own! Lord of St. Osyth's!" he exclaimed.

"You have heard the news, then," said the young man, throwing himself from the saddle, "let my horse be cared for; and you, John Lynch, come hither. I must speak with you."

He passed through the shop into an inner room, followed by the smith. Their conference lasted for nearly an hour, and when they emerged from the dingy little parlour, Reginald's brow was much clearer than before.

"Yes, sir," said John Lynch, continuing the conversation as he patted the horse's arched neck, and scanned him with the admiring eye of a connoisseur, "by the plan we have arranged, there won't be a yard of coast between this and Bolt Head left unsearched. And as I have been fixed here for nearly six months, I shall just give up the shop to my brother for a time, and go on the tramp myself. Six months is too long to be confined to one place."

" That's right, John," said Reginald, " you are worth any six of the rest on a scent of this kind. Send me the earliest intelligence, and above all—lose no time. I would be off myself, but I must pay some deference to appearances. Good bye!"

CHAPTER VI.

THE INQUEST.—REGINALD TRIES AN EXPERI-
MENT.—A PEEP OUT OF THE WINDOW.

ON his return home Reginald found that
the coroner had arrived, and was making
his formal inquisition into the cause of the
death of Mr. Hawkshawe and Lady Clarissa.

As the present head of the family was in
London at the time of the catastrophe, his
evidence could throw no light upon the
business, and was therefore not required,
further than to identify the bodies. He
had not seen them before, and turned heart-
sick at the horrid spectacle.

The business was quickly over. A verdict
of accidental death was returned; and then
the coroner and his myrmidons departed,

and left the undertakers to perform their ghastly office.

No question had been raised as to how the bodies of Lady Clarissa and her son happened to be in the spot where they were found, as the suite of rooms occupied by the old lady was on the lower storey of the wing that had been destroyed, and it seemed natural that Mr. Hawkshawe should either have been paying a visit to his mother, as he frequently did, or that he had rushed to her rescue on the first alarm of fire, and perished with her in the flames.

A more searching inquest was, however, to be held into the cause of their death; though in place of a jury of bumpkins, one keen and sorrowing mind would alone be called upon to give the verdict.

After a short rest, Reginald summoned Oliver, and bade him accompany him to the ruins, and point out the exact place where his father's corpse had been found.

They clambered over heaps of smouldering walls, where a couple of firemen were still keeping watch lest the flames should break out afresh, and stopped at a spot where a considerable quantity of the *débris* had been dug out.

By a gesture, Oliver signified to his master that this was the place, but his heart was too full to suffer him to speak.

"What is all this?" asked Reginald, pointing to some pieces of metal and half-fused glass that lay about.

"It's some of the queer things belonging to the old monks, I believe, sir," replied Oliver. "There was a row of their cells just above her ladyship's apartments, and many strange machines and vessels of different kinds I have been told were locked up in one of them."

"Chemical apparatus!" muttered Reginald, with a compressed pale lip, while he cast a scrutinizing glance around. Something like the bars of a fire-grate caught his eye. He pulled the object out, and within it found a few ashes, and a crucible. He placed the latter in his pocket, unseen by Oliver, and returned to the library.

Having placed the crucible under lock and key, Reginald wandered about the room, trying to guess what Ellen's occupations had been on the day of his departure.

The piano stood open. The music on the desk was his favourite piece. By the side of it lay a handkerchief of Ellen's quite damp. Had she been weeping? There was her work-basket, with her work thrown carelessly upon it, as though she had got tired of that employment.

Two or three books were taken down from the shelves, and left on the table. That was not like Ellen, for she always returned the books to their places. And, most startling evidence of all, there was her writing desk, unlocked and open, just as she had left it, when, in a fit of penitence, she had taken Frank Willoughby's portrait out of it.

That she had been suddenly and violently intruded upon he could have no doubt; the open desk, and the miniature on the floor, were proofs of that. He locked the desk, wrapped the little bunch of keys in paper, sealed it with his coat of arms, and directed it to Ellen; and when Oliver entered to entreat his master to take some dinner, he gave him the packet, with strict injunctions to deliver it only to Miss Maynard, or, in case of her death, to her attorney.

"How is that old coach-horse?" asked Reginald, as Oliver was clearing the dinner-table.

"Just the same, I believe, sir," he replied. "I think John was going to ask your leave to shoot it, sir."

"Tell him to bring me the key of the stables, and a lantern," said Reginald; "I will go presently and look at it."

After all the household had retired to bed, a light gleamed through the window of the loose box in which the old horse was lying. Reginald was mixing a white powder with some water in one of those equine pap ladles by means of which medicine is administered to horses.

" Now, poor old fellow," he said, as he raised the horse's head, " I trust this will prove harmless, if it does not end thy sufferings more quickly than a bullet."

The animal swallowed the draught, and Reginald, placing the lantern so that its light fell directly upon the subject of his experiment, leaned with folded arms against the manger, watching the effect of the potion.

Lady Clarissa was right in saying she had not forgotten the recipe for making that deadly poison. The horse lay quiet for a few minutes, then sprang to his feet, and fell dead.

The next morning the groom reported that the horse had died during the night, and Reginald gave orders, and saw them carried out, that the carcass should be buried, without flaying, in a deep pit. The disorder of which the creature died was, he said, highly infectious, and he would suffer no man's life to be risked for the sake of a horse's hide. To prevent the cupidity of the groom or any of the helpers leading them into danger, he caused a quantity of vitriol to be poured over the carcass, and the pit was then filled up.

"Is it not strange," observed Mrs. Sweetman, as she and Oliver sat at tea that afternoon, " Master Reginald could think of the old carriage horse, and run half over the country after Miss Maynard, which I feel quite sure was what he went about yesterday, Mr. Oliver, and he has never once asked whether poor Mrs. Hawkshawe is alive or dead? I suppose he thought if she'd have been burnt to death, too, he'd have heard of it."

"Have you finished your tea?" asked Oliver.

"Pretty near," replied the housekeeper; "but that's no answer to what I said. What do you think of it?"

"When you've finished your tea, ma'am, just come with me, and I'll show you a sight," said Oliver.

The promise of a "sight" has great power over the uncultivated female mind. Mrs. Sweetman's last cup was drained in a hurry, and she scarcely stopped to lock up her tea-caddy, before she announced to Oliver that she was ready, and he conducted her to a window that overlooked the garden.

"Well I never!" was the good lady's first exclamation. "Who ever would have thought it?"

"Ah! Mrs. Sweetman," said the old man,

with glistening eyes, " there's a good heart there—a noble heart! He's been wandering about with her for these two hours, just as you see him now."

The spectacle that had so excited Mrs. Sweetman's astonishment was that of Reginald and his poor, half-idiotic stepmother.

He was leading her about the garden, gathering flowers for her, and smiling sadly at her infantile expressions of delight at their beauty and fragrance. He watched her as tenderly as a mother would her child; bore with her whims and vagaries without a single glance of weariness or impatience; and strove, not unsuccessfully, to bow his hasty and manly mood to her timid and childish one.

Often the old frightened look would come over her face; and she would stare round in terror, as though she expected to see Lady Clarissa, or to hear her crabbed keeper reprove her for indulging in any amusement, or to be chilled to stone by a glance of the hard, cold eye. Then Reginald would hold her to his heart, and warm her into life again, and smooth her brown hair caressingly, and seem to whisper words of comfort. When she smiled confidingly in his face, he looked pleased and happy, and tried to divert her feeble thoughts to some other object.

"We have been here long enough, Mrs. Sweetman," said Oliver. "I could not refrain from showing you how much you were mistaken in Master Reginald; but it is not right to watch one's masters."

"I could watch him for hours," replied the housekeeper, wiping her eyes, "if I could only see for crying. And I'm sure there's no harm in looking at him now, God bless him!"

"He would not like it, ma'am," said

Oliver. "Besides which it would be a bad example if the other servants found us watching."

The last argument was conclusive, for Mrs. Sweetman entertained very exalted notions of her own dignity, and the duty that was incumbent on her of setting an irreproachable example to those under her orders.

When Reginald rang for tea, Oliver brought a message from Mrs. Grimston, the keeper, who wished to know if she should fetch Mrs. Hawkshawe to her own rooms. At the mention of this woman's name the poor lunatic clung to her step-son, and begged him not to let them take her away.

"Don't be frightened," said he, soothingly; "she shall not take you away. You shall stop with me, and I'll send Mrs. Grimston away, and you shall never see her again."

"Won't you send away the other one too?" said Mrs. Hawkshawe. "The old one—don't you know?"

And she pointed significantly across the table, and moved her eyes up by furtive starts as she used to do to Lady Clarissa's face.

"She is gone," replied Reginald; "she is dead. You will never see her again."

"Oh! I am so glad!" cried the lunatic, clapping her hands. "Then she can't make me look at her any more! And she can't look at me! I'm so glad! Is she buried?"

"Not yet," replied Reginald. "She'll be buried in a few days."

"Make haste and bury her," she whispered in his ear. "She's so tough, and so wicked, that she'll get up again if you don't."

"She shall not hurt you if she does,"

replied Reginald. "Tell that person," he said to Oliver, intimating Mrs. Grimston by a glance, "that I will speak with her presently, and desire Mrs. Sweetman to come here."

When the housekeeper entered, she was surprised to find Mrs. Hawkshawe (in a flurry of delight at the importance of the office entrusted to her) actually presiding at the tea-table.

It is true Reginald sat by her side, and guided her hand, lest she should scald herself with the boiling liquid; it is true also that he had to exercise a sharp *surveillance* over the other parts of the operation, or one cup might have been filled with cream and the other with sugar; but the idea was to her the same, *she* was making tea— *she* was being useful.

"Sit down, Mrs. Sweetman," said Reginald. "I have sent for you to ask a favour of you, which I do not think you will refuse."

"Indeed, sir, you may be sure I won't, if it is anything that lies in my power to do," replied the housekeeper.

"I find that Mrs. Hawkshawe's maid has behaved in a manner that is not at all what it should be," said Reginald, "and I shall be much obliged to you if you will undertake the office until I can find some one else. She will give you very little trouble, and in a few days I will take her to some more cheerful place."

"I'll do what I can, sir," replied the housekeeper, looking very anxious; "and as I said before, sir, if it's anything that I *can* do, you have only to say the word, as in duty bound. But I'm not over strong, sir, by reason I'm not so young as I was."

"Have you ever heard that any strength was required?" asked Reginald.

"No. sir, I can't say I have exactly," replied Mrs. Sweetman. "But I *have* heard of tantrums."

"The irritability caused by vexatious and unnecessary interference, that is all," said Reginald. "With kind and gentle treatment there is the utmost docility. Take my place here for ten minutes, and you will be able to judge for yourself. You will give Mrs. Sweetman a cup of tea, won't you, dear?"

"Oh, yes, yes," cried Mrs. Hawkshawe, pleased as a child at the notice he took of her, and the freedom he allowed. "Sit down, Mrs. Sweetman, sit down. I think I remember *you*," she added, staring at her visitor with a pained expression, "a long— long time ago!"

"You are forgetting the tea, dear," said Reginald, patting her face between his hands, and kissing her on the forehead. "I dare say you remember Mrs.

Sweetman, for she is a very old friend of ours ; so don't keep her waiting for her tea."

Having thus turned her poor brain from a dangerous subject, and set it on a right track, Reginald went out to speak to Mrs. Grimston.

The good old housekeeper was so deeply affected by her master's tender care of his unfortunate stepmother, that she could not restrain her tears. Mrs. Hawkshawe looked at her half in fear, half in curiosity, and pulled her handkerchief from her face.

It was years since she had seen a tear in human eye, nor had she shed one herself since she lost her reason. The sight moved her strangely. Wild convulsive sobs heaved her bosom, and she continued to stare yearningly in the old woman's kindly face and streaming eyes, while yet no "fellowly drops" moistened her own parched eye-balls.

Mrs. Sweetman read in that pallid up-
turned face and those dry, bitter sobs, such
a passionate appeal for tender, womanly
sympathy, that she folded the poor lunatic
to her broad bosom, and held her there in
a close embrace. Then the dried-up well-
springs of that suffering and tortured
heart once more overflowed,—with a
violent gush at first, and passionate
throes, but gradually calming down till
the sobs came at longer and longer
intervals, and at last she slept.

Reginald held but a very brief colloquy
with Mrs. Grimston. He told her he had
no doubt she had performed her office to
the best of her ability, but being convinced that Mrs. Hawkshawe's case required a different mode of treatment, he
should dispense with her future services,
and requested her to leave the house the
following morning as early as convenient,
as her late charge had so great a dread of

her, that he thought it advisable she should not see her again.

The woman attempted explanations and remonstrances, and finding that plan of no avail, had recourse to another line of tactics—pretended to shed tears, and talked of her long and faithful services. Without any harshness, Reginald gave her plainly to understand that all this was of no use; and having paid her what wages she demanded, without any investigation of the correctness of her claim, left her with imperative injunctions to depart in the morning.

Mrs. Sweetman's kind heart having been completely gained by the unfortunate lady, Reginald found no difficulty in prevailing upon her to undertake the post left vacant by Mrs. Grimston's dismissal.

The plan he proposed offered many in-ducements besides, as he intended (if his opinion were supported by medical advice)

that Mrs. Hawkshawe should be removed
from St. Osyth's, and travel about,
wherever the doctors might think it
desirable.

CHAPTER VII.

A MEETING AT THE GRAVE BY THE SEA.

A WEEK after the fire the double funeral took place. Reginald saw the remains of his father and grandmother consigned to the family vault, and when all was over he retreated to the lonely strip of beach, and shed a few bitter tears on the storm-beaten pile of stones beneath which his mother lay buried.

He thought of the sweet voice that had recited over her the same prayers that he had just heard read by the clergyman, and his proud heart was subdued. He leaned his brow against the rock, and prayed fervently and with humble spirit that Ellen might be saved from danger.

A touch on the shoulder aroused him. It was John Lynch, his dark face expressing wild excitement, and his chest heaving from the speed with which he had descended the cliff. Reginald grasped his hand, and uttered the one word, "Safe!"

"Ay—ay—safe and well," replied the smith. "What has happened to her I cannot tell; but I've found her; and that, I suppose, is all you want."

"Are you sure you were not mistaken? Are you *quite* sure it was she?" asked Reginald, eagerly.

"Did you ever know me to forget any face I had once taken notice of?" returned the smith, with a smile of irony—"and *her* face too! Why anybody could remember *that*."

"And where is she?" inquired Reginald, "Tell me the whole tale from beginning to end, as you used to do when I was a boy, John Lynch. Come—sit down, old friend, and don't miss a word of it."

They sat side by side upon a shelf of rock, and Reginald rested his cheek upon his hand, and his elbow on his knee, and gave himself up to the delight of listening to a tale of deeper interest than had ever held him silent and breathless in his boyish years.

"I told you," began the gipsy, "that I would be off upon the search myself, so I dressed myself in travelling trim, as you see," glancing down upon the ragged costume of a beggar, "and skirted along the coast. Plenty of shipwrecks I heard of, but no little boat, come ashore with a lady in it. I had no luck for five days; but yesterday, as I was prowling along a wide stretch of beach down in Devonshire, what should I see but a small boat lying above high water mark, bottom upwards! I didn't know her

at first in that position, but still there was
a something about her that made me go
nearer. Sure enough, it was your honour's
little Wild-duck!"

" You are *positive* you saw Miss Maynard
safe and well?" said Reginald, drawing the
breath through his closed teeth.

" That I did, and no mistake," replied the
smith.

" Then go on," said Reginald.

" When I saw that boat I *was* confounded,"
continued the smith; " but then I sees she
could not have got where she lay unless
she'd been hauled up; and, thinks I, the
same hands that hauled up the boat would
be able to save the young lady; and then I
thought of the life-belt, and mighty glad
was I to see the marks of a large dog's feet
on the sand. Off I sets to the nearest village,
and on my way I met one of our people who
told me he thought he had got a trace of
her. He had heard of a lady being at a

farm-house about two miles off the sea, and he went begging to the house, but couldn't get a sight of her, because he saw the master, and he's so charitable, he never turns a beggar away empty, so there was no pretence for making a row, and bringing the folks out of doors. Well, as I had got Jem Bryce's experience to guide me, I made him show me the farm, and then I skulked about till I saw the master go out, and a fine Scotch sheep dog with him, and after that I saw the missus busy in the garden. I seized the opportunity, and cut away round to the back door, where I had seen a vinegar-faced servant maid just before. I knocked first, and then set up a dismal story about my wife and eight small children, all ill of the ague, with nothing to eat, and no money to pay for doctor or physic. Just as I expected, the cross maid came out, and began calling me a gipsy thief, and all manner of names. But of course I wouldn't stir for

S—2

that. It was just what I wanted; and the more she scolded, the more I whined; till at last the parlour-door opened, and who should come out but Miss Maynard herself! She was wrapped in a shawl, and looked very pale, and so weak she was obliged to hold by the wall, as she came along the passage. She said something to the servant that sounded like a reproof, but her voice was so faint I could not catch the words. And then she came forward and gave me a half-crown. Here it is," he continued, showing it suspended by a ribbon round his neck, "and here it shall remain as long as I live. I bored a hole in it as I came back here by the express train last night. And now that's all the story, Master Reginald, and I hope you are satisfied with what I have done."

"Satisfied!" repeated Reginald, "my good friend, I am more than satisfied. I am grateful—I am delighted! One more favour I shall ask of you. To change that dress, and go with me to-morrow to show me the house. I have arranged all my affairs here in such a way that I can leave at a minute's notice. When you have got your own clothes on, my friend, come to the house and ask for me. We can then arrange about the trains and so forth."

He stood up, and remained for a few moments silent, with his eyes fixed on the ground. Then he extended one hand to the smith, and laid the other upon the cairn.

" You have removed a mountain from my breast, John," he said, " and when I forget your kindness, I shall have forgotten her whom we laid here in her last home. I may not have many more opportunities of speaking to you before I go, but be sure if I die on the field of battle, and have time to think at all, I shall remember your friendship. God bless you, John!"

He pressed his hand, turned quickly, and sprang up the rocky path.

"And God bless *you!*" said the smith, looking after him, "though as for not seeing me again, I don't quite know about that. I should not like a soldier's life, there's too much confinement, and too many rules, and too many orders to suit my constitution. But something in the sutler line would do very well, I fancy; and there's so many rascals take to that trade, I don't see why I should not try it too. And then I can keep an eye upon him."

After this soliloquy, the smith followed Reginald up the cliff, but before reaching the hermitage he turned off into a less-defined and more difficult track that led round the rock into the ravine.

CHAPTER VIII.

A TRUE GENTLEMAN.

ON the second evening after Ellen's escape from the Priory, the inmates of a farm-house on the Devonshire coast were assembled for evening prayer, in the large and comfortable parlour. The utmost order and decorum prevailed, for the master was respected, as much as he was beloved by his dependents.

Joseph Franklyn made no pretension to be a "gentleman farmer." He kept neither hounds nor hunters;—he did not even join the hunt;—but he *was* a gentleman for all that, and no occupation or mere outward

environment could have made him otherwise.

His face bore a singular resemblance to
the portraits of Melancthon, and expressed
a delicacy and refinement which his homely
farmer's dress rather enhanced by the con-
trast. His head was lofty—as with such a
face it must of necessity be—and the fine
hair, turning grey and falling off at the
temples, suffered the whole contour to be
visible—a sight that would have filled a
phrenologist with rapture.

He read the appointed chapter in a simple
and unassuming style, but in a voice of extraordinary sweetness, and with an earnest-
ness that never failed to rivet the attention
of his hearers.

His wife sat beside him with great dignity, and felt proud of her husband, though
she was weak enough—and a sad weakness
it was—to fancy that no one but herself
could see through his homely and unassum-

ing exterior, and appreciate the sterling
goodness of his character. She did not
comprehend that others, as well as herself,
must see that such a man as she had the
happiness to call husband would ennoble
any station of life. To her—in her own
private judgment—he was a gentleman in
the best sense of the word; refined in
thought and feeling—deeply, but unobtru-
sively religious; just, charitable, and true.
No coarse expression, no outburst of anger,
ever sullied his lips. The drinking bouts of
the neighbouring farmers had no attractions
for him; and while the best that his house
contained in cellar or larder was set before
them when they came under his own roof,
he systematically refrained, on all possible
occasions, from joining in their parties, which
were never considered to have been properly
and hospitably concluded unless every male
guest went away considerably the worse for
liquor. Yet, with the fullest appreciation of

his worth, Mrs. Franklyn did not give others credit for the same discernment, but thought that, to all the world besides herself, he was a mere plain farmer. Nevertheless, in her inmost heart she was proud of him, as she ought to be, and as no persons were present whose superior education or position might, to her foolish fancy, give them a right to sneer at him, she gave herself up with her whole soul to her devotions. At the close of the usual prayer Mr. Franklyn added a short extemporaneous one, for those who had been exposed to the "pelting of the pitiless storm" upon the treacherous sea, and his wife responded "Amen" in a broken voice.

"Go to bed, love," said Mr. Franklyn, kissing his wife, after the servants had dispersed, "you look sadly tired. I shall just step down to the beach again, to see if there is anything to be done. But don't you sit up. I'll take the key."

"You talk of stepping down to the beach,

as if it were only a two minutes' walk, instead of a long two miles," said his wife.

"Nay, nay, love," he interrupted, smiling, "not more than a mile and a half."

"Well, whatever it is," said his wife, "you have been down three times to-day already, and surely that is enough."

"I shall feel much more comfortable if I go again," he replied. "It is all very well to pray for the sufferers under a comfortable roof, and safe from all danger; but to my way of thinking such prayers are an insult to Providence, unless we follow them up by *doing* as well, whatever lies in our power to do."

"I see you are determined to go," said Mrs. Franklyn, "so it's no use to argue with you. But pray take Richard with you. It is so late to go alone along that dreary road."

"Richard is tired, love," returned Mr. Franklyn.

"He has not had so much to tire him as

you have, dear," replied she; "and the long and the short of it is, that if you go for your own pleasure, Richard must go for mine; for if you go by yourself, I shall be miserable till you are safe back again."

"Well, well," said her husband, "Richard shall go; so make your mind easy."

The man was not very willing to leave the bright kitchen fire for the dreary night out of doors; but to accompany such a master for the satisfaction of so kind a mistress, he concealed any feeling of reluctance, and started off without a word.

The moon was shining bright when they reached the shore.

"There beant nought on the water, maister," said Richard, in his broad west country dialect.

"No," responded his master, scanning the expanse of the rolling sea with more attention, "I am thankful to see no signs of wreck. But the damage must have been fearful in many parts."

"What's the dog about?" said Richard, pointing to the Scotch sheep dog, which had just dashed into the waves with a wild cry.

"He has found something," exclaimed Mr. Franklyn, running down the sands. "Good heavens! It is a human body!"

"And there be a booat, too," said the man, "turned roight over!"

Mr. Franklyn ran into the water to assist the noble dog in bringing the drowned person ashore. It was a woman with long brown hair that floated on the water like sea-weed. She was perfectly insensible, but as the boat was so near, and she was supported by a swimming belt, it seemed possible that life might be not yet extinct. At considerable risk of being swept away by the tumultuous waves, the master and dog brought the inanimate body to the dry beach, while Richard had contrived to do nearly the same by the boat.

"Never mind the boat!" cried Mr. Franklyn. "Come here, Richard, and help me to carry this woman to the house."

"Lor, sir!" said Richard, "she be dead. It beant no mortal use to carry a copse up to the house. Best leave her safe on the sands, and send the folks with a cart for her. They'll hold the crowner's quest in your house, and give the missus a world of trouble."

"Dead or alive, she rests under my roof this night," said the master, resolutely, "and if you will not carry her, I will. She is warm yet, and I feel sure that she still lives."

"Lor! do'ee though?" said the man, now really interested in the fate of the drowned person. "Give her to I, sir. I can carry her best by myself. Thee beant over strong."

This was true. Mr. Franklyn was a slightly made, and rather delicate man, but he would have overtasked his strength to perform a duty. The clown, who was a giant in strength and limbs, took the insensible girl in his arms like a baby, and carried her with ease, holding her close to him, that his warmth might help to restore her.

The dog ran on before, and by his scratching and barking had aroused every one in the house before his master presented himself. Mrs. Franklyn was sitting up till her husband's return, and had fallen asleep by the fire; but when she opened the door, and found the dog alone, and in a state of violent excitement, she drew the very natural inference that some calamity had happened, and uttered a shriek that brought all the servants down stairs in alarm. In a few minutes the sound of her husband's voice re-assured her.

"All's right, Eliza!" he shouted, "make up the fire! We are bringing some one home!"

All was hurry and bustle in a moment. The bellows were at work, blankets were fetched, and water was set on to boil, by the time that the master entered, followed by the stalwart carter, bearing his dripping charge. She was laid before the fire, and while Mrs. Franklyn and her maids divested the seemingly lifeless girl of her clothes, and wrapped her in hot blankets, the other man was sent for a doctor. Richard meanwhile reposed himself in the parlour, and Mr. Franklyn changed his apparel, which was wetted completely through by the sea water.

"May I come in?" said the master, tapping at the kitchen door. On receiving an answer in the affirmative, he entered. "Are there any signs of life?" he asked.

"There is warmth about her heart and

stomach," replied his wife, "and just now I thought I felt a slight movement of the pulse. Oh! Joseph!" she added, pressing his hand, "how thankful I am that you would not let me persuade you to stay at home to-night!"

"That will do, dear," said he, returning the pressure with interest. "I wish the doctor would come."

Mrs. Franklyn neglected nothing that seemed likely to assist in restoring the sufferer;—piles of blankets, bottles of hot water, mustard plasters to the feet and stomach, till at length a faint respiration was discoverable, and by the time the surgeon arrived, the patient had even swallowed a teaspoonful of wine. After some hours of careful attendance, he pronounced that her recovery was no longer doubtful. She was put into bed, and left to sleep.

Early the next morning he came again.

The patient was too weak to speak, but she opened her eyes and looked at him, smiled faintly at Mrs. Franklyn, seemed grateful for the kindness she received, took some nourishment, and slept again.

"It is strange that she should be out on the sea, alone in that little boat," said Mr. Franklyn, as they talked the matter over with the doctor down stairs.

"She is quite a lady," said his wife, "I can see that from her clothes."

"Have you found out her name?" asked the surgeon.

"Maynard," replied Mrs. Franklyn, "Ellen Maynard is marked on her pocket-handkerchief, and E. M. or E. Maynard on her linen."

"Indeed!" exclaimed Mr. Henderson, taking a newspaper from his pocket, "then I think I have a clue to the discovery of her identity. Look here, Franklyn! there was a Miss Maynard, a governess, supposed to have been killed at St. Osyth's, in that dreadful fire, when Mr. Hawkshawe and his mother Lady Clarissa were burnt to death. Here is the evidence before the coroner. Miss Maynard is missing. What is more probable than that the poor girl, frightened out of her senses by the fire, should get into a boat, and so be carried out to sea, and by God's Providence, cast ashore just on the very spot that you, you good Samaritan, had taken under your charge!"

And he clapped his friend on the shoulder as he spoke.

"And I tried all I could to keep him at home!" said Mrs. Franklyn, with a quivering lip.

"Hush!" whispered her husband. "I think you are quite right in your conjecture, Mr. Henderson; it accounts for her being out by herself; and it is not likely that two young ladies of the same name would be lost and found within fifty miles of each other in so short a time."

"Had we not better send and let them know she is safe?" suggested Mrs. Franklyn.

"Why, I think not," said the doctor, "as we have at present only strong presumptive evidence of her being the same lady. Besides she is not a member of the family, and in a day or two she will be able to act for herself."

So it was decided that nothing should be done in the matter, and Reginald was kept in suspense for some days longer till informed of Ellen's safety by his gipsy friend.

On the occasion of John Lynch's visit to the house, Ellen heard from the servant's words that there was a gipsy at the door, and for love of one who had some of the dark blood of that wild race in his veins, she crawled out to speak a word of kindness, if she had strength to utter it, and at all events to relieve his distress.

The next evening she persuaded her kind host and hostess to go to a meeting, which · she accidentally discovered they had been long engaged to attend. Before setting out Mrs. Franklyn had a fire lighted in the parlour to keep her company, and Ellen lay on the sofa, thinking sadly of the past, but not venturing to dream of the future.

She had asked no questions about the fire at St. Osyth's Priory, not feeling strong enough to bear the confirmation of her fears, and being also unwilling to subject herself to any questions for the present. It was growing dark, but the fire burned brightly, and she had just refused the servant's offer to bring candles. A nightingale was singing in a tall tree in

the garden, and the sweet sounds floated
in at the open window along with the
odours from the flower beds. She was
thinking of Reginald, when, attracted by
that magnetic sympathy which she had often
felt before, she raised her eyes to the
window, conscious that some one was
looking at her. It was Reginald's face—
seen for one moment, and gone the next.
A slight crunching of the gravel gave
evidence that her sight had not deceived
her. She tottered across the room, calling
his name. There was no answer. When
she reached the window no form was
visible; but as she turned away, her eye
was caught by a small packet lying on the
window-sill.* She brought it to the fire.
It was directed to her in Reginald's well-
known bold, rough characters. She
opened it — it was Frank Willoughby's
portrait, which she now recollected had
been left on the floor where Mr. Hawk-

shawe had flung it. Reginald had discovered her then—but how? A moment's
thought settled the question—the gipsy
beggar! Surely Reginald would write to
her! How strange that he should come in
that mysterious way, and disappear without
saying a word. Again she examined the
paper in which the portrait had been
wrapped—the poor portrait itself, I am
sorry to say, did not get a second glance.
In vain—there was not one word besides
the direction.

When Mr. and Mrs. Franklyn returned,
they found their invalid suffering from
considerable nervous irritability. The
next day she was worse, Mr. Henderson
was sent for, and pronounced it to be low
nervous fever. For several weeks she lay
between life and death, and when at length
the fever left her, she was so much
reduced, that her recovery was as tedious
as her illness.

CHAPTER IX.

LADY WILLOUGHBY ALTERS HER TACTICS;
AND MR. SMEDLEY TAKES A JOURNEY.

We must now return to Lady Willoughby, who, in the meanwhile, had spent her time in alternate rounds of fashionable dissipation, and fits of hysterics, and other complaints of the nerves and imagination.

On the arrival of every mail from the Crimea Mr. Smedley was so regularly summoned to attend her ladyship, that he began to think he might as well go without waiting to be sent for; and taking the postman's and errand boy's duties as well as his own, put Frank Willoughby's letter in one pocket, and the "Restorative Drops as before," in another.

He was heartily sick of her ladyship's whims and caprices; the case was wholly devoid of professional interest; and he would have given it up, but that he was thereby kept fully informed of Frank's movements and intentions, in which he felt a lively interest for the young man's sake; but still more for Ellen's. So he comforted himself by making Lady Willoughby pay well for her fits, and wrote again to Ellen, giving her all the gossip of the place, and the latest news of Frank, brought in quite incidentally. To his annoyance and vexation the letter was returned from the dead letter office.

He determined to set off as soon as his professional duties would allow, and make personal inquiries on the spot; but like many good resolves, whose execution depends upon some contingent " as soon as," this journey was deferred week after week.

Towards the end of September a letter arrived from Frank; and the doctor was sent for as a matter of course. Lady Willoughby was less hysterical than usual; but the doctor's quick eye detected that her thoughts were busy upon some project which she endeavoured to conceal from him. Instead of giving him her son's letter to read through as usual, she folded down a part, and handed it to him. What he *did* see gave him food enough for reflection.

"A very singular fellow joined ours a few weeks ago. His name is Reginald Hawkshawe, of an old family in Cornwall. He has lots of money, having just come into his property on his father's death; but he don't know how to spend it, I can see. He lives in the most abstemious manner, and seems to care

much more for his horse than for himself. He's not a miser, though, by any
means, as more than one of our mess can
testify. He will pay off any young
fellow's gambling debts, on his giving a
solemn promise not to touch cards or dice
again. They call it taking Hawkshawe's
pledge. The men adore him already, and
no wonder, for he is always doing something to improve their condition. Then
his strength is so tremendous, and he
never spares it. He will often bring a
wounded man back from the trenches after
undergoing fatigue that would have
knocked up anybody else. I was quite
done up two nights ago, so that I
stumbled and fell; and before I could
recover my legs Hawkshawe had got me
on his back, and so marched me close up
to our tents. He said he hoped the Fates
would accept it in lieu of his having to
bring me off wounded. He has taken me

under his special protection, and when it is my turn in the trenches he always spends a great part of the time with me. Notwithstanding his willingness to work, and the courage and spirit he displays when there is any skirmishing going forward, he is generally very melancholy. I think he has been disappointed in love; though how any girl could do other than accept such a fine, handsome fellow, I cannot imagine—and so rich too! She may be dead; but he is not the sort of fellow one can ask questions of, so I only guess at it. He has got all my love affair out of me, and Ellen's name is as pat on his tongue as possible. Do you know, mother, I think I was wrong to promise to give her up. Hawkshawe has set it in such a strong light before me. that I really begin to think it would be a rascally shame to desert her. Give my kind regards to Mr. Smedley, and ask him to send me her address. Hawkshawe has been talking to me again. Excuse the incoherency of this letter; it is so difficult to write at all, that nothing but the most desperate resolution carries one through. I have put no dates, for they would only confuse you. Sometimes a week has elapsed between the beginning of a sentence and the end of it.

"Hawkshawe has been at me again about Ellen. He says I never deserve a happy moment if I break my word with her. I fancy I can see a little into his . own mystery through all this. I think he has broken faith with some one, and she has killed herself, or gone mad, or died, or something, and that is why he is so melancholy, and urges me so strongly not to bring a life-long reproach upon my conscience. I told him I had run through so much money, that I was very much embarrassed, and you wished me to mend my . fortune by a rich marriage; but he said that such a girl as Ellen would love me for myself, and not for my riches or position— in fact, one might suppose he had known her for years, he understands her disposition so thoroughly from my account of her. Poor fellow! his melancholy grows upon him. He has a firm belief that he will never return to England; but it is not *that* that weighs on his mind, for he came out on purpose to get killed. *I* don't think the metal is dug out of the mine that will wound him, for he seems to bear a charmed life, and we never hear of a man getting shot when he wishes for it. I wish you would ascertain whether Ellen has had any money left her. Hawkshawe throws out such strange hints on the subject."

The first line of the next paragraph, which Lady Willoughby had turned under, was just visible, and Mr. Smedley did not scruple to read it:—

"I have just found out, by his hints, what that strange fellow Hawkshawe means. He has made his "—— Mr. Smedley had no difficulty in filling up the blank with the word " will," and adding " in Ellen's favour;" but he was aided by a little previous knowledge.

" He writes in high spirits," remarked Mr. Smedley, returning the letter; " and I do not wonder that your ladyship is so much better, after receiving such a cheering epistle."

" I have been thinking a great deal about what the dear boy says respecting Miss Maynard," said the lady; " and really you know, doctor, I feel that I *ought* to study his wishes. One can never be sure," she added, putting her handkerchief to her eyes, " that each request may not be the last. Besides, Miss Maynard, poor dear girl! was always such an immense favourite of mine, that I really feel quite anxious about her. Can you tell me her address, doctor? I wonder she has never written to me."

"I do not know where she is at present, madam," he replied. "I wrote to her at her former address, more than six weeks ago, and the letter was returned."

"Dear me! how very provoking!" cried her ladyship, with the eagerness of a whist-player, fearful of losing the odd trick; "we must find her out! Where was she when you wrote before?"

"She has sent me only one letter since she went away," said the doctor, evading a direct reply, "and it is evident she has left her then residence for good, or my last letter would not have been returned."

"Sweet girl!" sighed the lady, "we *must* find her."

"I am very anxious to know what has become of her," said Mr. Smedley, "and I think I may be able to do so; in which case I will inform your ladyship. I am delighted to see you so much better, as I am compelled by urgent business to be absent for two or three days. I must now take my leave, for I have several visits to pay. A holiday is such an unusual event with me, that it requires a deal of preparation. Good morning, madam." And he bowed himself out.

He trotted briskly as long as he was within sight of the drawing-room windows, but as soon as he had passed the lodge gates he suffered his horse to walk, while many thoughts occupied his brain.

It may be remembered that the only letter from Ellen that had reached his hands was written immediately after Reginald's discovery of his father's perfidy respecting the former one, and it was natural that her pen should write something of what her heart felt so strongly.

She therefore told Mr. Smedley that she

occupied the position of instructress to Mr.
Hawkshawe's son, whose education had been
totally neglected, though he was far beyond
the usual age for being under female tuition;
and then she spoke warmly of the noble
disposition which he evinced. At the time
he supposed all this to refer to a boy of
fourteen, or perhaps sixteen; but now
strange doubts arose in his mind. He
fancied she had said " Mr. Hawkshawe's *only*
son," but of that he could not be sure till
he had read her letter again.

Who then was this Hawkshawe who had
suddenly appeared in the Crimea, and in
Frank Willoughby's regiment — suffering
under deep melancholy—interesting himself in Frank's fate—drawing out his love
secret — persuading him not to abandon
Ellen—and finally leaving her some property, which he felt convinced was the conclusion of the sentence of which he had
read the first line? There was a singular

mystery in all this; and the only solution appeared to be in the existence of a character that was almost chimerical for its disinterestedness.

"Ay, ay," he soliloquized, as he rode gently along, "there's some money in prospect for Ellen, I am sure, and a good lump, too, or the old cat would not be so anxious about it. But this Hawkshawe puzzles me. Can it be the father? I must read her letter again, and see what light that will throw on the matter."

Setting spurs to his horse he was quickly at home. The cautious wording of Ellen's letter did not enable him to gather much from it, but it certainly was, "only son."

"Then this Crimean hero must be Hawkshawe, senior," he muttered, "or the deuce is in it. What! Ellen Maynard governess to a man old enough to hold a commission in her Majesty's army! No—I'll not believe that. But I can't wait for the morning

10—2

train. I'll start to-night. It will save me some hours, and I cannot rest till I have sifted this business to the bottom."

In passing through London Mr. Smedley called on Mrs. Mason; but that good lady had heard nothing of Miss Maynard since she was spirited away by that tall, dark man, with the fierce eyes. He started off by the Great Western, and the following day reached the village to which she had desired him to address his letter. On inquiring for John Lynch, he was told that he had left the place some months back, and was supposed to have gone to the Crimea.

His next question was respecting a Miss Maynard.

"Miss Maynard!" repeated his informant, the landlord of the village inn. "Why, mayhap that's the young lady that was burnt to death at St. Osyth's."

"Burnt to death!" exclaimed Mr. Smedley. "Good heavens! Poor, dear girl! How dreadful! How and when did this happen?"

"Missus!" shouted the man, calling to his better half, "wasn't it Miss Maynard as was burnt at St. Osyth's?"

"Lawks sake, mun, no," she replied, appearing from the rear of the house; "it wasn't known for sartain sure that she were burnt. 'Cos you see, sir," curtseying to the strange gentleman, "her copse was never found."

"Is nothing known of her, then?" inquired Mr. Smedley.

"Nothing for sartain, sir," was the reply; "for you see when the Priory was burnt, and Mr. Hawkshawe and his mother were both killed, it made a great confusion, and in the midst of it, the young lady disappeared."

"Mr. Hawkshawe and his mother burnt!" exclaimed Mr. Smedley. "I have heard nothing of that. What Mr. Hawkshawe was it?"

"The father of the present gentleman, sir," replied the woman.

"And was no search made for Miss Maynard?" inquired Mr. Smedley.

"Oh yes, sir," she replied. "They were digging in the ruins for days, I've been told. Mr. Reginald was up in London at the time of the fire, but he came down as quick as steam could go, and I'm sure it was a sight to see him the very night he got home, come galloping like mad to have a consultation with John Lynch, the blacksmith."

"By the same token," chimed in the husband, "John gave up his shop to his brother, and went off that very same night, and has never been seen in these parts since."

"Is his brother still living here?" inquired Mr. Smedley.

"Yes, sir," replied the man, "down at the smithy yonder."

"Is he a dark-faced fellow that looks like a gipsy?" was Mr. Smedley's next inquiry.

"He looks like what he is then, I reckon," said the landlord, grinning.

"I can make nothing of him," said Mr. Smedley. "I asked him several questions just now, and could get no satisfactory reply. He seems half a fool."

"Not he, sir, begging your pardon," said the landlord; "he's as 'cute a chap as there is between here and Lunnon. If he know's what you want, and why you want it, I daresay he'll tell you all about it."

"I'll try him again," said the doctor, dubiously, "though I fear it's of no use; and in the meantime I will trouble you, ma'am, to get me a chop, or something of that sort, ready for my dinner."

"Perhaps your honour would like a chicken, sir?" said the landlady.

"Anything you please, ma'am," returned Mr. Smedley; "only let it be ready as soon as possible."

Mr. Smedley found the smith smoking his pipe at the door of his shop, and he began, " I think, my friend, you can give me more information respecting Miss Maynard than any one about here, if you are disposed to do so. I have no evil intentions towards the young lady; indeed I am one of her oldest friends, and I was a friend of her father's before her."

" Be you a lawyer?" asked the man, sullenly.

" No, I am a surgeon—a doctor," replied Mr. Smedley.

" What name?" asked the smith.

" Smedley," replied the doctor.

" Why didn't you say so before?" exclaimed the smith. " Didn't you send a letter here once for her?"

" Certainly I did," replied the doctor, " or else I should not have dreamt of inquiring for her here."

" No, not at a smith's shop, I daresay,"

returned the smith. "It ain't much of a place for a young lady. Come in, sir, and I'll tell you where she is."

Mr. Smedley followed him into the little parlour, and there the gipsy wrote, in a much better hand than could have been expected, Mr. Franklyn's name and address.

"You see, sir," said he, giving the paper to the doctor, "I don't like answering questions unless I know why they are asked. It saves a deal of trouble sometimes, and I've got so into the way of it that I scarcely ever answer straight for'ards. Now that I know you are all right, I'll tell you what I know about her. When the Priory was burnt—at least one wing of it—Miss Maynard made her escape in a small boat, and as the weather was stormy she was drifted about all night and all the next day, and then she was picked up by this Mr. Franklyn. She has been at his house

ever since, very ill, and near dying;
but she's getting better now; so if you are a
doctor you can't do better than go to her."

"I *did* intend going to St. Osyth's to
make inquiries there," said Mr. Smedley;
" but I suppose they could tell me nothing
more than you have already said."

" Not so much neither by a long chalk,"
replied the smith; " they know nothing
about her."

" There is one more question that I
should like · to ask," said the doctor,
" What was Miss Maynard's occupation at
the Priory?"

" You'd better ask herself, sir," said Joe
Lynch, with a sly smile; " how should I
know anything about it?"

" Humph!" said the old gentleman, per-
ceiving that Joe had fallen back upon his
" know-nothing" system; " perhaps then
you can tell me how many sons the late
Mr. Hawkshawe had?"

"Can't say, sir," replied the gipsy, assuming an expression of hopeless stupidity; "never heard."

Mr. Smedley laughed, thanked Joe for his information, and returned to the inn to dinner.

Being out of the way of the railroad, Mr. Smedley hired a conveyance, and late in the evening arrived at Mr. Franklyn's door.

At the sound of wheels the master came out, expecting to see one of his neighbours, and prepared to warn him to speak gently, lest he should disturb the invalid.

"I believe, sir," said the doctor, in a low voice, "that you have a young lady, Miss Maynard, under your roof?"

"I have, sir," replied the farmer, "and if you are a friend of hers, I am heartily glad to see you. She has been very ill, and we have not been able to obtain from

her the name and address of any of
her relations, so that it has been quite
impossible to communicate with them."

"She has no relations, poor girl," said
the doctor. "I am only an old family
friend. Has she never mentioned the name
of Smedley?"

"That is the only name which she has
mentioned," replied the farmer, "and she
has several times wished Mr. Smedley were
here. Have I the pleasure of speaking to
him now?"

"Yes," replied the doctor, agreeably
struck by the gentlemanly address and
manners of Mr. Franklyn; "and, as a
medical man, I hope I may be admitted to
see her."

"I beg your pardon for not asking you
to alight sooner, sir," said the farmer, while
a bright blush overspread his mild features.
"My reason for detaining you here was
that I feared the sound of your voice might

reach Miss Maynard, and agitate her, for she is still very weak."

"I'd better ask a few questions before I present myself," said Mr. Smedley, stepping out of the chaise.

"Shall I wait, sir?" asked the postillion.

"Yes; I want you to take me to an inn," said Mr. Smedley.

"No! no! decidedly no!" cried Mr. Franklyn. "With your good leave, sir, you sleep here to-night. I cannot suffer you to go to the inn. Have you any luggage?"

"A carpet-bag," he replied; "but really —the trouble—what will your good lady say?"

"I daren't venture to think of what she would say if I were to let you go," said the farmer, with his soft sweet laugh; and grasping the bag he led the way into the parlour. "Miss Maynard is in what my wife calls her drawing-room," he said, closing

the door, and placing an arm-chair for his
visitor, "and I think there is now no danger
of her hearing your voice."

At Mr. Smedley's request he gave a full
account of the way in which he had discovered Ellen, and of the illness into which
she had fallen, after the doctor had pronounced her convalescent. In Mr. Henderson's opinion, he added, this had been
caused by some nervous shock or fright,
though they had never found out that she
had been subjected to any. It was true
she had been left alone on the evening when
she was attacked by this fever, and might
have had some slight alarm, but she would
not own it.

"She is so feeble that a very trifling
cause is sufficient to upset her," continued
Mr. Franklyn; "for instance, a few weeks
ago, when she had recovered so far as to be
able to walk in the garden, she was thrown
into excessive agitation by the sound of an

Eolian harp which my son had placed in his window. She imagined it to be a token of death to some friend, and could scarcely be convinced that the sound had a perfectly natural cause. And even though we satisfied her on that point, she had a relapse in consequence of the fright. I do not know whether a pleasurable emotion would be hurtful to her, but it will be best to keep on the safe side, and give her due notice before she sees you."

"Quite right—quite right," said the doctor. "By-the-bye, my dear sir, you must have been at considerable expense all this time. How has Miss Maynard been off for money? Her lawyer is a neighbour of mine, and if she had drawn upon him I am sure he would have told me. It was but the other day he was expressing to me his astonishment at not having heard from her."

"She had some money," replied Mr.

Franklyn, " and we have received some since from an anonymous friend. We have been rather in a dilemma about this, and I shall be glad to profit by your advice. This letter," he said, taking one from his pocket-book, " arrived here a few days after Miss Maynard was taken ill the first time. It contained Bank of England notes to the amount of a hundred pounds. Read it, sir."

Mr. Smedley adjusted his spectacles, and read as follows:—

" Sir,—The enclosed sum of £100 is placed in your hands by a friend of Miss Maynard's, for her use, and to remunerate you for your expenses on her behalf. For your kindness to her, all to whom she is dear will ever remain your grateful debtors. You must use your own discretion whether or not to inform her of this communication. The sender of it would prefer that it should be kept secret from her; but if any incon-

venience or unpleasantness should arise in
consequence, you are at liberty to tell her
that it comes from some property which she
will shortly inherit."

"What would you advise me to do?"
asked the farmer.

"What *have* you done?" was the counter-
question.

"I have placed the money with my
banker," said the farmer, "but have not
mentioned the subject to Miss Maynard, as
her medical attendant says she must be
kept perfectly quiet, and we feared that the
mystery of this business might agitate her.
When she has expressed a wish to write to
her lawyer for supplies, we have dissuaded
her, and prevailed upon her to put it off.
She *must*, eventually, be told of this money
having been sent, or we shall be placed in
the awkward predicament of receiving
thanks and gratitude for services for which
we have been paid at least fourfold, besides

the dishonesty of appropriating the whole of the money."

"*Property she will shortly inherit!*" said Mr. Smedley to himself, looking at the letter again. "Reginald Hawkshawe again for twenty pounds! Well, sir," he continued aloud, "I will, if you please, see our patient as soon as convenient. Perhaps you would just mention that an *elderly* friend wishes to see her. The idea of a staid old fellow is not so agitating to a young lady as the anticipation of a pair of military spurs clanking across the hall."

"I'll act upon your hint, sir," said Mr. Franklyn, as he quitted the room.

In a few minutes he returned, and conducted his guest into another apartment. Ellen started up from the sofa with a cry of delight, and, greatly to the old gentleman's astonishment, and perhaps also to her own, threw her arms round his neck, and sobbed like a child upon his shoulder.

"I thought it was you," she said, "but how did you find me out? Oh, I am so glad to see you! Not that I have anything but the kindest treatment here; you will not think I mean otherwise, dear, kind friends?" And she took Mr. and Mrs Franklyn's hands. "You will not suspect me of such base ingratitude after all that you have done for me; but it is so pleasant to see an old familiar face—the only one that remained unchanged amid the wreck of fortune!"

"Nay—not the only one," said the good doctor, watching the effect produced by his words, as he would have watched the effect of some delicate operation; "there may have been others, or at least *another* that remained unchanged, though too far away for you to distinguish it."

"Possibly," said Ellen, in a subdued voice, "but I do not know—I have not heard."

Instead of the rosy blush which such an allusion might have been expected to call up, even on her pale check, there was an expression of pained embarrassment and shrinking.

"Hawkshawe again!" thought the doctor; "does she love him then? Yet if so, why did they not come to an understanding? I must get to the bottom of all this mystery."

He sat beside Ellen on the sofa, and after about half an hour's chat, ordered her off to bed. She had given him only a very brief account of the manner of quitting St. Osyth's Priory. She was dreadfully alarmed, she said, on the night of the fire, and got into a boat in which she was carried out to sea, and drifted about till cast ashore near Mr. Franklyn's house. Mr. Smedley saw very plainly that there was a great deal more which she left untold, but reserved all cross-questioning till the next day. He spent another hour in pleasant conversation with

Mr. and Mrs. Franklyn, joined in their
evening devotions, and retired to rest,
pleased with the successful result of his
journey, delighted with his new friends, but
sorely puzzled concerning Ellen's relations
with the Hawkshawe family.

CHAPTER X.

EXPLANATIONS AND BLUNDERS.

THE day after his arrival at Mr. Franklyn's
the doctor took the opportunity of being
alone with Ellen to say, rather suddenly,
"Pray, my dear, what was the age of your
pupil at St. Osyth's?"

"Oh, pray don't ask me, Mr. Smedley!"
replied Ellen, showing now that if she did
not blush the evening before it was not for
want of blood to crimson her neck and
face; "it was really quite shocking; but
I was completely trepanned into it."

"What was shocking, my dear young
lady? How were you trepanned? And

who trepanned you?" inquired the doctor, eagerly.

"No, no, I cannot tell you anything about it," she replied, turning pale and sick with horror, as her mind ran rapidly over all the circumstances, ending with the terrible conviction that poor Mrs. Hawkshawe had been poisoned, and probably burnt, to hide the deed of blood; "I cannot tell a part without relating the whole, and there are some things that must not be revealed, which I try not even to think of. Perhaps it was only a hideous dream. I'll try to believe so."

She uttered this in a low hurried tone, half speaking to herself.

"Can you tell me," she continued, but without looking at him, "whether any lives were lost in the fire?"

"Yes, Mr. Hawkshawe and his mother were both killed," he replied.

"Mr. Hawkshawe and Lady Clarissa!"

repeated Ellen, looking up with a face in
which horror and delight struggled strangely
for mastery ; "then their blood cannot
come upon my hands, say what I may.
Heaven's justice has overtaken them! And
Mrs. Hawkshawe—is she dead too?"

"No," said Mr. Smedley; "I was told
that her son had placed her under the care
of a person who had been the housekeeper
for some years, and that she was travelling
about for the benefit of her health. What
is amiss with her?"

"She is insane," said Ellen, with a dis-
tracted air, which might easily be mistaken
for deep sadness. She was thinking how
to frame a question respecting Reginald.
but Mr. Smedley interpreted her look and
tone very differently.

"Insanity in the family!" he thought,
"and therefore they would not marry.
Quite right—quite proper—but, poor young
souls! what a heavy trial!" He had, as he

thought, solved the mystery at last. "It is odd," said the doctor aloud, "that you should ask me about the incidents connected with the fire, when I only learnt them myself since I came into this part of the country. The catastrophe was doubtless detailed in the daily papers, but I have not often leisure to read them, and the home news has little attraction, beside the latest intelligence from the Crimea."

"I have not dared to ask," replied Ellen, "for I dreaded to hear something that would have brought a burthen upon my conscience like the guilt of blood."

"Will you not confide in me?" said the old gentleman, taking her hand. "An experienced head may guide you better than the quick impulses of your own young brain, however conscientious in its judgments. Believe me, my dear, I do not ask this out of curiosity, but from a wish to serve you."

"Of that I am sure," she replied, "and under a solemn promise of secrecy will tell you all."

"I give you my word never to divulge what you are going to say," replied the doctor.

She then related all that had occurred since the period of her arrival in London; only suppressing any allusion to Reginald's attachment to her, as well as to the feelings which she could no longer disguise from herself that she bore towards him. In the course of the narrative Mr. Smedley learnt that the insane Mrs. Hawkshawe was not Reginald's mother; and consequently, that his supposed solution of the mystery was not the correct one.

"Off the scent again!" he thought: "but I am glad *that* was not the reason. All may go right yet."

He sneered of course at the boding of the Grey Maiden, but instantly connected it with the fact of her suffering a relapse at the sound of an Eolian harp, and concluded, rightly enough, that she had feared it was the Death Wail for Reginald.

The account of the preparation of the poison interested him deeply; though he could not guess, from her description, of what nature it might be.

" Let us hope that the baleful secret expired with her," he said; "and now, my love, try to banish from your mind all recollection of these horrible events. Heaven has taken their punishment into its own hands, and as the crime was not actually perpetrated, the knowledge of guilt need not oppress you. The son appears to be a noble fellow, and will atone amply for his father's faults."

" He is, indeed, all that is good and noble," said Ellen, with enthusiasm.

" Then you do not hate him for his father's sins?" suggested the doctor.

"Oh, no! that would be gross injustice," said Ellen. "Besides, what do I not owe to his kindness and forethought!"

"Yes—he's doubtless a fine fellow," said Mr. Smedley, "and makes a good officer, it seems."

"Is he, then," faltered Ellen, trying to look indifferent—"is he—has he been—mentioned—in the papers?"

"Yes—favourably mentioned, more than once," replied the doctor. "I have heard of him besides through a private channel. He is, singular to say, in the same regiment as Frank Willoughby, and has cemented a strong friendship with him. He has paid off Frank's gambling debts, shares and relieves his duty in the trenches, and watches over him like a brother. I am glad you have no dislike to him, for, being such fast friends, he is sure to be invited to

Willoughby Court, and you could not avoid seeing him."

Mr. Smedley was obliged to desist, for the victim of his cruel experiment was falling from her chair.

"You have talked too much," he said, assisting her to the sofa, and holding a glass of wine to her lips. "Now you must lie quite still for an hour, and to remove the temptation to talk out of your reach, I'll go and have a chat with our good friend Mr. Franklyn."

In the afternoon Ellen was better and stronger, and when Mr. Smedley, after a long consultation with the other surgeon, urged the advisability of change of scene, and also the benefit likely to be derived from her native air, adding (by way of experiment) Lady Willoughby's affectionate inquiries, she readily agreed to his proposal to place herself for a few weeks under the care of his housekeeper, a respectable, elderly widow, whose nursing talents were celebrated in the little town. He was rather puzzled by the pleased reception she gave to Lady Willoughby's overtures.

"Am I mistaken about Reginald?" said the doctor to himself; "and is she still fond of Frank? Who the deuce can read what is passing in a woman's mind, or comprehend her motives of action? Not I!"

With which soliloquy he left the question for time to settle.

Nothing occurred worth recording during the next three days, to which the good old doctor prolonged his stay at the farm. By that time Ellen's health was so much restored that she was able to undertake the journey as far as London, where she would remain with Mrs. Mason for a day, or longer, if needful.

When the time of her departure was

fixed, she consulted Mr. Smedley on the proper means of remunerating her hospitable entertainers for all the care they had bestowed upon her, and the expense they must have incurred on her account. Without telling her of the money that had been sent by her anonymous friend, who, he felt more and more convinced, was no other than Reginald Hawkshawe, he assured her that all that had been satisfactorily and handsomely arranged between her hosts and himself, and that when she was able to attend to business she should audit the accounts, and make all straight with him. Glad to escape from any unnecessary trouble, she gratefully adopted his arrangement, whatever it might be.

Ellen wept at parting with the kind friends whom Providence had raised up for her in her time of need, but promised herself the pleasure of speedily paying them another visit. The journey to London was ·

accomplished with less fatigue than might
have been anticipated; and after one night
spent at Mrs. Mason's, who was overjoyed
to see her, she continued her route to her
native town.

CHAPTER XI.

LADY WILLOUGHBY CARRIES OUT HER PLANS.

It was barely a year since Ellen had left her native place, but what a change had come over her feelings in that time! How the placid and childish love which she had felt towards Frank Willoughby had been swept away by the tyrannous control of a far sterner and loftier character than his;—a control that she *could not* resist, which mastered her whole being and her every faculty, and compelled her love and admiration, in spite of all her efforts to assure herself that she was still faithful to her early attachment.

"The place is not much altered," observed Mr. Smedley, as they drove in from the railway station, in his gig.   .

"To me it seems very much changed," she replied; "I cannot point out where or how, only that it seems smaller."

"Your ideas have become more expanded," said he, with a smile; "I dare say you will not find Willoughby Court looking less stately than usual."

"I shall not very soon be able to bear the fatigue of going there, I fear," said Ellen.

"Nor would I advise it before her ladyship calls upon you, my dear," returned Mr. Smedley. "We must keep up our dignity, and she owes you the *amende honorable*."

"I cannot quite understand her," said Ellen, with a half-contemptuous smile. "Has there been any news of my father's unworthy cousin having realized a fortune in Australia, and died, leaving it to me? Nothing less could fully account for the change in Lady Willoughby's behaviour."

"She is a very weak and capricious woman," said the doctor, "and we must never expect to find sufficient motives for the conduct of such people. By Jove! the most reasonable of your sex are difficult enough to understand, without wearing one's brains to shreds in the effort to discover what such simpletons as my lady are driving at."

"You are in one of your complimentary moods, I see, doctor," said Ellen; "but pray keep a pretty speech to pronounce as I cross your threshold, for here we are at the door."

"Do you find any change here, my dear young lady?" asked Mr. Smedley.

"Yes," she replied, smiling affectionately at his pleased face as he handed her out, " yes—it looks more home-like and comfortable than ever!"

Her first impression proved to be correct, for she was at once installed in full possession of every luxury afforded by the doctor's comfortable, but not ostentatious establishment.

As soon as Lady Willoughby heard that Ellen was in the town, she drove over to see her.

The first interview was highly diplomatic on both sides; though Ellen kept wholly on the defensive or negative system, keeping quiet and saying little, on the plea of her weak health. By this means the visitor had far the greater share of the conversation to herself, and Ellen was enabled to form some guess at the nature of her manœuvres, and their object. There was a superabundance of professions of personal regard, and fulsome terms of endearment; but not the slightest allusion to the rela-

tionship in which they might one day stand
towards each other. There were many
very friendly plans for the fut—visitsure,
to the metropolis, introductions to society
under her ladyship's chaperonage; but
no word of the preparations for her
marriage.

Ellen's heart was no longer interested in
the matter, and therefore her head was cool
and collected enough to mark all these
details with considerable accuracy, and to
draw her own conclusions from them. The
result of these was that Lady Willoughby
wished to keep on perfectly good terms
with her, but to pledge herself to nothing;
in order that, on some turn of fate of which
Ellen could not guess the nature, she
might be free either to press the marriage,
or to treat it as a subject that had never
been under serious discussion.

Ellen felt no compunctious visitings of
conscience at meeting her visitor in her

own spirit, using against her the same weapons which she employed, and obtaining, through Frank's letters to his mother, intelligence of Reginald.

And what of Frank, in the meanwhile? How far was he implicated in his mother's disingenuous proceedings? On that point she could not wholly satisfy herself. Lady Willoughby read portions of Frank's letters to her, but they related entirely to the movements of the army, and their sufferings during the terrible winter of '54 and '55. Sometimes Ellen was given to understand, by a sudden stop and some humming and ha-ing, that there was an allusion to herself which the reader thought it best to suppress. But Ellen was too clear-sighted not to see through the manœuvre which let the existence of this allusion be guessed at; while by not reading it aloud, the artful woman could not be accused of encouraging, or even acknowledging the engagement, should circumstances render it politic to break it off.

"Yes!" thought Ellen, "she wishes to keep alive my affection for her son, that I may be ready to marry him, in case some change of fortune should render it desirable. She does not care for the other side of the question. It is nothing to her that the hopes she strives to nourish may be crushed, and that with them my heart may be broken, and my life blighted. Poverty and sorrow may be *my* lot. And this is her friendship!"

But by far the most interesting portions of Frank's letters were those in which he spoke of his friend Hawkshawe. Ellen had kept secret from Lady Willoughby the name of the family in which she had resided during the year of her absence, leaving her even ignorant that she had been in a situation at all; and she had asked Mr. Smedley to observe a similar silence upon this topic. The concealment was much facilitated by her ladyship, whose purpose it served to ignore all such matters in case the marriage should take place. She therefore asked no questions, and Ellen was much amused to find that it had been industriously circulated throughout the town that she had been on a visit to some friends of Mr. Smedley's in Devonshire. This was easily traceable to the doctor's having made some casual remark in Lady Willoughby's presence, touching " Our friends the Franklyns."

" I do not think," said Ellen, as she talked the affair over with her medical friend, " that I become an accomplice in a falsehood by not denying a silly report. I shall therefore let it pass. It is none of my inventing, and I am not bound to refute it. If people will talk of what does not concern them, they must expect sometimes to hear falsehoods as well as truth."

"But this is not wholly a falsehood," said the doctor. "You certainly *were* at the Franklyns for some time; and as to their being friends of mine, I trust they will continue so to the end of the chapter."

"Then I shall let this report go uncontradicted," replied Ellen. "It will serve my turn, by saving me the trouble of repelling impertinent inquiries, made under the mask of friendship."

"How bitter you are against our towns-folks!" cried the doctor. "I did not imagine there was so much causticity in your composition."

"My memory is not so short that I should set much value on their present professions," replied Ellen. "I see that they are all led by the same idea, that I am about to become possessed of some property. I wish it would make haste and come!"

"Perhaps it cannot come to you before the death of its actual possessor," observed

the doctor, turning away, and looking out
of the window.

A thought flashed across her brain—
could it be? The doctor was known to be
wealthy—he was a bachelor, without any
near relative—he treated her like a father.

"If it be so," said Ellen, "I wish that
wish un-wished with all my heart."

"That I am sure you do," said the
doctor; and he ran down stairs to a
patient whom he saw coming to the door.
"Poor girl!" he muttered, "she little
guesses at the truth!"

But she had guessed at a fiction which
had the salutary effect of giving repose to
her mind, during which her bodily health
and strength were rapidly restored.

During that long and dreadful winter she
had constant news of Reginald through the
unconscious Lady Willoughby, with whom
she was by this time on the most friendly
terms; and she was sustained also by a super-

stitious belief that Reginald would not die without the Death Wail being heard by her.

On the terrible night of her escape from St. Osyth's the mournful sounds had accompanied her for miles on her lonely voyage, and would they fail to warn her of *his* death?

In the spring Ellen agreed to accompany Lady Willoughby to London, to be introduced into society. This, at least, was her ostensible motive; but the real one was that she might have the opportunity of meeting with officers home on sick leave, who had seen and spoken to Reginald. Many such she met with, but her appetite for such news was insatiable, and she went more and more into society to gather intelligence, of which she never wearied.

One morning a letter arrived from Frank; and Ellen, with ill-concealed anxiety, awaited the usual reading of a portion of it. Lady Willoughby read it, folded it up, and looked thoughtfully at the direction.

"Good news, I hope?" said Ellen, at length.

"Oh yes! Excellent!" replied her lady-ship; "but, my dear child, I don't know how to read it to you! It's positively all about yourself; and you know it does seem so odd to write a love-letter through another person! I told him you were staying at Smedley's, and had promised to come to town with me for the season, and the poor fellow is quite wild with joy. He is coming home on sick leave, having been slightly wounded, and not very well in other respects; and he begs me to have everything in readiness that the marriage may take place a week after his arrival!"

"What marriage?" asked Ellen, coldly.

"You little prude!" said her ladyship, playfully pinching her cheek; "pretending not to know, indeed! However, as the bride-elect is just your height and figure, we will get you to let the milliners take your measure for the *trousseau*."

" I should think," said Ellen, calmly, " that Captain Willoughby will be too much occupied in re-establishing his health, so as to be able to return to his duty, to think of getting married in such a hurry."

" Marriage will be the cure, my love," replied her ladyship, laughing. " The naughty boy's principal ailment is love-sickness, and there is no remedy like matrimony for that complaint."

" And can he suppose that the lady will feel flattered at his deserting his country's cause for her sake?" said Ellen.

" Of course she will!" replied her lady-ship. " Women are always flattered in proportion to the extent of the sacrifice that is made for them. But I must leave Frank to plead his cause for himself. I have too much to do now in preparing for his return."

Would Ellen's feelings have been so completely Spartan on this occasion if she had preserved her attachment to Frank Willoughby? Let us hope that they would, though they would probably have taken a very different appearance. Instead of expressing a quiet opinion, as if for another person, she would have shed tears of mortification and regret. She would have written letters of remonstrance to meet him at every stage, urging him to return to the scene of duty and of danger, and vowing, if he persisted in his shameful retreat, to enter a convent, and spend the remainder of her days in penance for having been the cause of his disgrace.

Lady Willoughby did not half like the way in which her young guest fell into her own plan of treating the engagement as a thing that had never had an existence. She felt herself foiled with her own weapons, by one whom she had always considered a

complete novice. Perhaps Ellen was only
taking a little girlish revenge; perhaps she
was only coquetting a little, in order to be
more ardently wooed afterwards. But how
if she had by any means obtained an inti-
mation of the principal news contained in
Frank's letter—that Hawkshawe was killed,
and that she—Ellen—was left sole in-
heritress of his large property? Smedley
was the only person who could know anything of the matter; the question therefore
was, "Had Ellen received a letter from
Smedley that morning?" On inquiry she
learnt that Miss Maynard had had no
letters that morning; so, anxiously rumi-
nating, she drove off to the War-Office to
obtain a confirmation of Reginald Hawkshawe's death.

We must do Frank the justice to say
that his letter was very different from what
his mother chose to represent it. He told
her he was quite doubled up with grief at

the loss of his friend; that his restlessness interfered with the healing of his wound; and that he had applied for, and obtained a promise of leave to return home to recruit his health. He only once alluded to the subject which his foolish mother said was the single theme of his letter. " Ellen is now wealthy," he said; "but I would rather have such a friend as Hawkshawe than a hundred wives, each with a hundred fortunes." In a postscript he added, " I forgot to tell you the nature of my wound, and I suppose you will be anxious to know. It is only a Minié ball through my right leg, but being close to the knee, it is awkward. Hawkshawe carried me back to the ambulance amid a perfect hail of rifle balls, so that it seemed a miracle that we were not both killed. He then ran back to the trenches, and it was in the command of *my* men, and doing *my* duty, that he lost his life. The service and the world altogether could far better have spared *me*."

Foolish Lady Willoughby! With your caprices, and sophistications, and worldly-mindedness, you had made a tolerable clearance of all honesty of heart from your own nature; otherwise you would have comprehended that the sight of Frank's letter, with its expressions of genuine and natural feeling, would have impressed Ellen far more favourably towards him than the silly romance which you invented.

Ellen, disappointed at not hearing Reginald's name mentioned, took the *Times* to her favourite seat in the conservatory, and searched for news of him there. Too soon she found it in the list of killed! There could be no doubt about it. The details were too circumstantial. He had fallen in defending an advanced post, from which the allies were driven back for some hours. The next day they had recovered the ground, and Captain Hawkshawe's body was found, stripped by the Cossacks, and the head frightfully mutilated by a cannon ball. Ellen read it all. She did not shriek, nor weep, nor faint, but sat like one who was stunned by a heavy blow. She knew nothing of the flight of time; she felt nothing but a dull weight of misery, and a sort of dread that when she was aroused it would be to suffer tortures more excruciating than she could bear. And so she sat for hours, till roused by Lady Willoughby's voice, calling her to take a drive.

"Why, my sweet pet!" exclaimed her ladyship, fresh from the agreeable confirmation of the news of Hawkshawe's death, "what ails you? How pale you look!"

"I have been asleep, I think," replied Ellen, passing her hand over her burning forehead. "I shall be better soon. Yes, I'll be ready directly."

Her maid attired her, and she went

mechanically to the carriage. The fresh air of Hyde Park revived her, but the unceasing turmoil, and the (to her then state of mind) ghastly phantasmagoria of faces decked in unmeaning smiles, that swept past like the files of antic shapes which often flit before the eyes in childhood, oppressed and annoyed her, and she longed for the pure air, the solitude, and the perfect quiet of the garden at St. Osyth's. But that wish and its attendant recollections were quickly and peremptorily banished, for behind them lay tears and shrieks of agony, which that was no place nor time to indulge in.

Be the story of the Spartan boy and his fox reality or fable, it shadows forth a terrible truth. How many poor mortals, who bear a calm brow and a smiling lip, carry their fox carefully hidden in their bosoms, and feel it gnawing at their hearts even while they utter complimentary nothings to their merest acquaintances! With Ellen it was a strong instinct that first led her to conceal her fox; then when she could reflect at all, her reason approved what she had done, and she continued the same line of conduct.

She nerved herself to stoical endurance, looking forward, when she anticipated the future at all, to spending some time, perhaps the remainder of her life, under the peaceful shelter of Mr. Franklyn's roof. It was there that she had last seen Reginald, though the glimpse had been only momentary; and there she could mourn over his loss, unintruded upon by curious and impertinent questionings. The moderate sum which had been saved from the wreck of her father's property would suffice for her simple wants in such a home, though while with Lady Willoughby it only supplied her with pocket money.

She could not be said to have thought of

all this, but it passed vaguely through her mind as a consciousness that she could find a peaceful asylum when she chose to seek it. For the present, hateful as society and gaiety were to her, she went out more than ever, that she might meet with people who could tell her anything of Reginald. No one knew that she had ever seen him, and she schooled her looks and tones so successfully, that she was never suspected of being the deeply interested listener which she was.

CHAPTER XII.

WEALTH IS NOT ALWAYS WELCOME.

IT was about a week after the first news of Reginald's death had arrived, that a stranger sent in his name at an hour too early for ordinary callers, desiring to speak to Miss Maynard on business. Ellen felt nervous and frightened, she knew not why. She half dreaded, half hoped, to hear something about Reginald. While she hesitated, Lady Willoughby, for they were still lingering over the breakfast table, glanced at the card, and directed that the gentleman should be shown into that room.

"You will hardly like to see a stranger

alone," she added, half apologetically, to Ellen.

If Ellen thought differently she had not time to say so before the stranger was ushered in. His business was quickly explained. Premising that she had no doubt heard of the death of his late client, Reginald Hawkshawe, Esq., of Hawkshawe Castle, ——shire, and St. Osyth's Priory, Cornwall, he proceeded to state that the said gentleman had bequeathed to her the whole of his property, excepting the Hawkshawe estate, which was entailed, and that he was ready to place the will and other papers in the hands of her solicitor, unless she would honour him by leaving her affairs under his superintendence.

"Pray retain the papers, sir," said poor Ellen, and her voice sounded to herself as though it belonged to some one else, who was speaking at a distance under a vaulted roof; "they cannot be in better hands, I am sure. I will call on you in a few days, if it is necessary; but at present I am not well; I cannot talk about business."

" Do you wish me to prove the will?" asked the lawyer.

" Whatever you like—whatever is necessary," said Ellen, to whose ears the word *will* —Reginald's will—was like a touch on a bare nerve. "I cannot speak more now; I feel really ill."

And she staggered from the room.

" Poor thing!" exclaimed Lady Willoughby, " she is quite overcome by the sudden news; and · pray excuse the remark, but I think, sir, you communicated it *rather* abruptly."

" Was not Miss Maynard aware of Captain Hawkshawe's death?" asked the gentleman, in some consternation.

" Possibly," said Lady Willoughby; " I know nothing to the contrary; but no doubt she must have seen it in the papers.

That, however, could not have affected her, for she did not know him. He was acquainted with her only through my son's description of her."

"Indeed!" said the lawyer, dubiously; for he had read Ellen's agitation very differently. "May I ask how long your son and Captain Hawkshawe were acquainted, madam?"

"I cannot tell exactly," replied her ladyship; "but it was some time last autumn."

"They went out to the Crimea together, I presume?" continued the lawyer.

"No; the regiment had been out six months before Captain Hawkshawe joined it," said Lady Willoughby.

The gentleman thanked her ladyship for answering his questions, and took his leave, wondering what all this might mean. The will had been made before Reginald left London for the East.

When Ellen reached her dressing-room she locked the [door, threw herself [on her knees, and tried to pray, and tried to weep. But her brain seemed hardened, and she had repressed her tears so long that not one blessed drop would flow to save her from madness, or cause the fiend that was griping at her throat to relax his merciless hold.

An organ in the street began to play. It had a sweet and plaintive tone, and it played an air that Reginald used to love. Her sobs subsided. She knelt with her head resting on a cushion, and her eyes wandering dreamily over the chintz pattern of the sofa cover, mechanically tracing out the flowers. A sense of freshness came over her soul, and when the music ceased, she raised her head, and found that the cushion was soaked with tears.

She wiped her eyes, and sat down to write a letter. Refreshed by that genial shower, a faint hope had raised itself in her heart.

"I do not believe that he is dead," she murmured to herself. "I am certain I should have heard the warning. If it was not heard at the Priory, I shall feel convinced that he still lives."

The letter she wrote was to Oliver, requesting him to inform her by return of post whether the Death Wail had been heard about the house since Mr. Reginald's departure. This letter she posted with her own hand, much to the astonishment of Lady Willoughby, who considered such an act anything but *comme il faut* in a young lady of fashion, and an heiress; but she was still more astonished when, three days after, Ellen received a letter directed in a stiff, old-fashioned hand, the contents of which seemed to give her great pleasure, though she maintained a profound silence on the subject. It was from Oliver, and ran thus:—

" HONOURED YOUNG LADY,—Thanks be
to God, there has been no sound of the
Wail since the night of the fire, which
makes me feel very sure that the dreadful
news we have heard from foreign parts is
not true, but quite otherwise. Distance
has nothing to do with the Wail, for it was
heard very plain for my late master's
brother, who died in India, which I am told
is a great way further off than where
Master Reginald is gone to.

" Please to excuse the liberty I take as
an old servant of the family for forty years,
to say how glad I am to hear that you are
safe and well, as this leaves all here at
present, thank God, and also we hear from
Mrs. Sweetman that our poor lady gets on
much better than could be expected, which
is all Master Reginald's doing. Nobody
thought any otherwise than that you had
been burnt to death, unless it was my
master—I mean Master Reginald, and he

sealed up your keys, and left them in my
care in case you should come here for your
clothes and things, which not hearing anything of you for so long a time, I never
thought would be likely to happen. I will
never believe that he is dead till I hear the
Wail, and when that time comes I hope I
may be permitted to lay my old head in the
corner of the churchyard. So no more at
present from your humble servant to
command, OLIVER CLARK."

After receiving this letter Ellen went
with a firmer heart to the solicitor, and
astonished him by saying she felt very
confident that Captain Hawkshawe still
lived. Not wishing, however, to be put into
a lunatic asylum, she refrained from com-
municating to him the grounds of this
belief. She desired him to act with
regard to the property exactly as he had
done before he received the report of
Reginald's death.

"But, my dear madam," said the lawyer, frowning in perplexity, "this is something beyond a report. Here are the proofs."

"I cannot look at them," said Ellen, turning away her head; "manage all as you have done till the expiration of one year. If he should not re-appear by that time——" Her voice failed her, and she stopped; then recovering her self-possession, she added in a decided tone, "Let me hear nothing of it till that time, if you please."

"But the entailed estate," said the lawyer; "you cannot put off the heir-at-law as you defer your own claims."

"Of course if you are satisfied with these proofs you must give that up," said Ellen. "I have no control over it. You must act for yourself. I may perhaps ask permission to go to St. Osyth's for a short time, but I am not sure."

"You have only your own permission to ask, Miss Maynard," returned the lawyer.

"I can go then when I will," said Ellen.

"Certainly," he replied; "but I must claim your attention to one point before you go, as there is a proviso in the will which it is important that you should be acquainted with. When you marry, the property is to be strictly settled on yourself."

"That is a very important proviso indeed!" said Ellen, with a hollow laugh, as she turned to depart.

CHAPTER XIII.

FRANK'S RETURN, AND MORE EXPLANATIONS.

On her return home Ellen could not but be aware of a certain briskness about the servants, as though something at once agreeable and important had happened. But as it could not concern Reginald, she felt no interest in it, and was ascending the stairs to her own apartment when the drawing-room door opened, and Lady Willoughby, seizing her by the hand, exclaimed, " Prepare for a delightful surprise!"

" Is he come back alive and well?" cried Ellen, clinging to the balusters for support.

"Yes, he is well—quite well," said her ladyship, "but frightfully thin; though looking so handsome!"

"Fool!" was the thought that shot through Ellen's mind, almost ere her tongue had spoken, "she does not mean Reginald!"

"Come in—come in! He is here in the drawing-room," said her ladyship.

"You are speaking of Captain Willoughby," said Ellen, as though she had just made a discovery; "how silly of me to make such a mistake!"

"Who *should* I mean but Frank?" said her ladyship. "Who *could* you be thinking of, you naughty girl?"

"It is immaterial," replied Ellen, calmly, as she accompanied Lady Willoughby into the drawing-room. "I was about to hope that your son is well, madam; but one cannot expect any officer to be in health, if he returns from the Crimea."

"He is much improved by his voyage,"

said her ladyship, biting her lip with vexation, "but he is far from well even yet."

Frank was lying on a sofa, but started up on their entrance, and advanced to meet Ellen as if about to clasp her in his arms; but she gave him her hand with an air of dignity that repelled all such familiarity. Her heart beat violently (as what young girl's would not?), but she preserved the outward appearance of composure.

"You are very much changed, Ellen!" said Frank.

"I can return the compliment, if it be one," she replied.

"I do not mean in appearance," said Frank, "but in manner."

"That change did not begin with me, Frank," she replied. "I appeal to your mother——" But Lady Willoughby had slipped out of the room. thinking they would get over the first explanations best without a witness. "However, as she is gone I will say nothing about her in her absence."

"What can have happened?" said Frank. "You are surely not the same Ellen that I used to know! She was all love and gentleness, while *you* are cold, severe, and stern. Tell me what I have done to make you change so suddenly."

"The change that it has taken a year and a half to accomplish, cannot be very sudden," said she.

"But your messages sent through my mother——"

"I have sent none," interrupted Ellen.

Frank bit his lip with an air of vexation.

"For the last six months I have not had a letter without one," said he.

"Then the less you say of conduct so disgraceful, the better," replied Ellen. "*I* am compelled, in justice to myself, to repeat

14—2

that I have never sent, nor even tacitly authorised the sending, of any message to you. And you, Frank," she continued, attacking him in return, " *you*—who wonder if I can be the Ellen of former years—can *you* be the generous-hearted Frank who was the playmate of my childhood? Would *he* have so soon forgotten the death of his best friend, and hurried home, under a false plea of indisposition, to clutch at that friend's wealth by means of an indelicately hasty marriage?—a marriage too with one whom he and his mother had both systematically slighted while she was poor?"

" There is something that wants clearing up here," said Frank, while his brow flushed, and his lip trembled; "and, though it's a dreadful thing to be compelled to blush for one's own mother, I very much fear, when all is made straight, and the saddle is put on the right horse, that is what it must

come to. You say that I systematically
slighted you when I knew you had lost
your parents and your fortune. Now, I
swear that I wrote dozens of letters to you.
Some I sent enclosed to my mother, some I
sent through the post. Those sent by post
were returned, and my mother assured me
that after the death of your parents you
desired our correspondence should cease,
and that you had broken off our engagement. I was involved in debt through
extravagance and betting, and I felt angry
with you, and turned sulky, and so the
matter rested. Then when Hawkshawe
came out, he got the whole affair from
me, I don't know how; and he saw it
all in a very different light, and said that
such a girl as I described you to be, would
not change her mind in that way. He said
it was very likely that when you lost your
fortune, you would throw up the engagement, to give me the power of retreating

handsomely, or of showing the sincerity of my affection by seeking you anew. I can't tell you half the arguments he used; but when he had worked upon me to such an extent that I was fully resolved upon seeking to renew our engagement, and had written to my mother begging her to find out where you were, he then told me he thought I was worthy of you, and that he would make us comfortable, and smooth away all family objections, by leaving his disposable property to you, having a strong presentiment that he should be killed."

"And when he was killed," said Ellen, reproachfully, "you sent a fulsome love-letter *at* me, through your mother, and scarcely mentioned the loss of your noble friend!"

"Did she read that letter to you? Did you see it?" he demanded, eagerly.

"No," replied Ellen, "it was too much even for *her* maternal vanity."

"Stay here till I come back," said Frank; "promise not to stir!"

"I will remain," said Ellen.

As Frank limped out of the room, Ellen wished she had spoken less harshly to him, and when he returned she was at the door to give him her arm to lean on.

"Thank you," he said, as he resumed his seat on the sofa, and with a slight contraction of the brow placed the wounded limb in a horizontal position. "I have got this *love-letter* from my mother. Read it, but I warn you there is nothing in it to flatter feminine vanity."

"How long has Lady Willoughby been aware of Reginald's intentions?" asked Ellen, when she had perused the letter.

"*Reginald's?*" repeated Frank, in amazement.

"Captain Hawkshawe's, I mean," said Ellen.

"She must have known them for six

months," replied Frank. "I told her as soon as he said it, because it was a proof what a good fellow he was, and I thought it would please her."

"You thought it would induce her to make inquiries after me," said Ellen.

"Well, perhaps so," he replied; "it's no use denying it. That *was* my motive. Hawkshawe advised it."

"This letter," said Ellen, looking over it again, "discloses many things to me, and not the least satisfactory of these disclosures is, that your affection for me is not what it used to be."

"My dearest girl! don't suppose that!" exclaimed Frank.

"I do not suppose it," said Ellen, "I *know* it; and I am glad to know it. It saves me the sorrow of inflicting pain on one whom I esteem so highly as yourself. Now, don't interrupt me, Frank, and don't remonstrate. You and I must be friends, and we must have no concealments from each other. Our youthful love is dead, or rather it has changed its character; or perhaps it never existed at all, except in our imaginations. But we are friends—we love one another as brother and sister, and if that fatal ˎwealth ever becomes really mine, I could never marry. Oh! Frank! Frank! can you not understand my meaning?"—and she covered her face with her hands, and wept abundantly—"that will is dated at the end of last June, before he quitted England!"

"Why then, he must have known you before he came out!" said Frank.

"Yes—and loved me," she replied, in a voice choked with sobs.

"And you loved him!" exclaimed Frank; "of course, you could not help it."

"I did," replied Ellen, "but he did not suspect it. It was not till he was gone that I knew it myself. He thought I loved you. I don't know how he found it all out, and that you were in the Crimea; but I am quite sure he knew it. He used to read the papers to me, and perhaps I showed some unusual interest when your regiment was mentioned. And he saw your portrait too, by accident."

"That explains his conduct when he was first introduced at our mess," said Frank. "He was very silent and reserved, though not at all shy or constrained; and he examined all our faces, as though he meant to paint our portraits, and at last he fixed upon me. I now understand the whole of his conduct. But, good Heavens! did any one ever hear of such disinterested affection! He seems to have delighted in sacrificing himself in every possible way to preserve me for your sake! And at last gets himself killed while doing my duty! Don't scorn me for these tears, Ellen. The oldest veteran in the army might shed them for such a cause, and I am weak with illness and my wound."

"I love you for shedding them, Frank," she replied; "they do you honour. But I cannot believe that Reginald is dead. Did you see the body that they called his?"

"Yes, I saw him," replied Frank, mournfully.

"Tell me *exactly* what the appearance was," said Ellen. "Do not hesitate for fear of grieving me. The report said that the head was mutilated by a cannon-ball. Was it so?"

"It was indeed," he replied, shuddering, as he recalled the horrid spectacle.

"Could you distinguish the features?" she inquired.

"No," replied Frank.

"And the body was stripped?" she continued.

"Yes," said Frank; "but his height was so remarkable——"

"Others might be as tall," interrupted Ellen. "And now I will tell you why I believe him to be still alive. There is a peculiar sound heard before a death occurs in his family, and it has not been heard since he went abroad. Do not look so incredulous, Frank," she continued; "I have heard it twice myself, and on both occasions a death immediately followed. You shall see a letter which I received to-day from an old servant, assuring me that the Death Wail has not been heard. However it may be, I am resolved not to touch the property for a year."

"In that I think you are quite right," returned Frank; "and I wish your comfortable superstition may prove correct."

"I believe it will. I am sure it will!" replied Ellen. "And you, too, will believe it when I tell you the whole story; but that cannot be yet."

"Why not?" inquired Frank. "We have two good hours to dinner-time."

"I cannot remain in this house any longer, Frank," she replied.

"Surely you are not so foolish as to run away because I am here!" said he.

"Not I, indeed," replied Ellen, with a faint smile; "but I must be hypocrite enough to make that my excuse. Your mother has been sufficiently punctilious on points of etiquette to put it out of her power to object. I shall accept an invitation that I received before anything was known about this property, from a delightful old maiden lady—Miss Brownlow. You must recollect her, I think. She used to visit the Eatons."

"I know her well," said Frank; "and I know she will not object to my coming to see you at her house."

"There, then, I will go," said Ellen.

"But you have not told me your reason for leaving my mother's house, Ellen. What is it, if not that I scare the proprieties?"

Ellen did not reply by words, but she looked at Frank's letter to his mother, and turned it round in her fingers.

"Ah! I see," said he, moodily; "of course you cannot like to live with her after that. And by making me and propriety the scape-goats, you avoid any disagreeable explanations, and a possible row, and hysterics, and all that sort of thing."

"Exactly," replied Ellen; "that is my object; and, Frank, I think it may be best to avoid telling Lady Willoughby of the explanations we have had. When I was first left poor and almost friendless, she chose to treat our engagement as a childish affair that could not be recognised by grown-up, sensible people; and when, about six months ago, she sought me out, and treated me with the most assiduous attention, my pride, as well as my altered feelings, made me take the cue from her former conduct. Mr. Smedley had dropped some hints of a fortune that was likely to come to me, and I imagined the dear old gentleman meant to make me his heiress, and that in the hope of making us happy, he had confided it to your mother. You may suppose that her friendship, based on such interested motives, was not very flattering to me. I accepted her overtures as a matter of policy and convenience to myself, because it was only through your letters to her that I could hear news of Reginald. You may be inclined to accuse me of acting with duplicity equal to her own in this; but I do not think the accusation would be just."

"No, no," said Frank; "I think you were quite right."

"Lady Willoughby," continued Ellen, "had definitively denied and annulled our engagement, as far as she could do so, and your long silence had confirmed her decision."

"But I wrote repeatedly, you know," he said, warmly.

"It was all the same, as far as I was concerned, because your mother suppressed your letters," said Ellen. "When she sought to renew her acquaintance with me she said not a word of renewing our engagement; and I think I was justified in treating it as a thing that had never existed."

"So you were," said Frank, with a sigh; "no one can blame you."

"I am glad you say so, because I am so anxious to retain your good opinion," said she.

"There is one thing, Ellen, that I cannot quite comprehend," said Frank. "How is it, that with all this weight of anxiety on your mind, you can go out to so many parties, and indulge in so much gaiety?"

"How do you know that I indulge in much gaiety?"

"My mother told me," replied Frank; "and warned me that I must not lose time, for you already have plenty of admirers; and when it becomes known that you have a large fortune as well, you will have offers of marriage by the dozen."

" And you listened to that prudent advice, and would have acted upon it?" said Ellen.

"Why," continued Frank, "you know I thought you still had an affection for me, and upon my word I was not aware, till you found it out and told me of it, that my feelings towards you had undergone the slightest change. And then, again, how could I suspect that Reginald knew anything about you before I told him? Could the wildest flight of imagination have guessed the truth? And Reginald told me, too, that he left all to you that my mother's objections might be removed. What *could* I think, you know, but that the best way to carry out his wishes was to get married at once?"

"That is satisfactory enough," said Ellen; "and I see that your conduct was perfectly natural, though rather hasty. And now I will tell you why I have 'indulged in gaiety.' It has been simply that I might meet and converse with officers from the Crimea who could tell me anything about Reginald. The gaiety has not been of the most exhilarating character, I can assure you."

"Poor girl!" said Frank, with glistening eyes. "I can well believe it! But now you will hear enough of him from me. I shall never tire of talking about him. Not a day passed without his performing some generous action, or doing good to some one, even to one of the enemy. One day we had had some skirmishing, and he, as usual, lent his gigantic strength to help in bringing our wounded men back. The place where we had been at it was a mile beyond our outposts, and the enemy had fallen back from it too. Well, just at dusk, Reginald came to me to borrow a lantern that I had got, so of course I asked what he wanted it for. And then he told me that among the Russians who were left dead where we had been fighting, there was an officer who was not dead, and who spoke English well. He told Reginald he had a young wife, and a little son a few weeks old, whom he had never seen. 'And now, perhaps,' he added, 'I never shall see him.' So Reginald bound up the Russian's wounded leg with his handkerchief, and whatever else he could lay his hands on, and placed him as comfortably as he could in a thicket, that our fellows might not carry him off as a prisoner, and now he wanted the lantern to find him, and help him on to his own people. I tried all I could to dissuade him, for I feared he might get shot; but he only smiled, and said, 'If

I am, Frank, I cannot die at a better time, nor in a better service. A man who is killed in battle, dies in the service of his country; but a man who is killed in the performance of an act of humanity, dies in the service of God. If I don't return, give my love to your wife—to Ellen Maynard—and may you both be happy!' Still I tried to keep him from going, but it was all of no use. I dare say you know how determined he was. I begged him to take some men with him, and bring the Russian back, for he would be well treated with us, though a prisoner; but he shook his head, and said, quite reproachfully, ' That young wife, Frank!' and turned to go. Then I said I would go with him."

"Dear Frank!" sobbed Ellen, amid her tears. "I was expecting that! I thought you would say so!"

"It was all of no use," continued Frank; "he would not suffer me to go. One, he said, could go with comparative safety, where two would be almost certain to run into destruction. Besides, he said, *I* had some one to live for, which made my life valuable; whereas *he* had nobody to care for him."

" What a mistake!" sighed Ellen.

" So the end of it all was that he would go alone," said Frank, "and alone he did go. He carried with him water, and brandy, and wine, and bread, besides the lantern and some bandages. I determined to keep watch till his return; but oh! you cannot imagine how weary a fellow feels after being on duty all the night before. I got a book and sat on the edge of my bed, and began to read : but I could not have been at it many minutes before I fell back fast asleep. The first thing that roused me was Reginald putting my legs upon the bed, for they were dangling over the side in a most uncomfortable way, and covering me

over with the blankets. I heaped all
manner of abuse upon myself for being
such a selfish brute as to sleep while he
was in danger; but he only laughed, and
assured me there had been no danger at
all.   He found the Russian officer just as
he left him, and the bandages had kept
pretty well in place.   He gave him bread
soaked in brandy, and then he got him on
his back, and carried him to the Russian
outposts.   The sentries were amazed, but
treated Reginald with great respect, when
their officer spoke to them ; and there
he left him, praying Heaven to give him
an opportunity of proving his gratitude.
There, now—can any one else tell you
such an anecdote of your Reginald?   Will
you not stay with me rather than go to
parties?"

"I shall not go to so many, certainly,"
replied Ellen; "but there is one at which
I shall meet a gentleman whom I very

much wish to see, and as it does not take place for a fortnight, perhaps you may be able to go too. You will be certain to have an invitation when it is known that you have returned. There is a great demand for Crimean heroes."

"It is fortunate for many of us that everybody does not judge our heroism by so high a standard as you do, Ellen," he replied, "or some who now get praise and honours, would only receive blame and contempt."

"I hope you will forgive me, Frank, for so misjudging you," said Ellen; "but it was owing to your mother having told me you were returning almost solely on account of—of—getting married, in fact."

"It's a very hard case," said Frank, "to be compelled to blush for one's mother; but I must own that I am heartily ashamed of mine. However, it's not the first time by many, so you need not feel uncomfortable about it. I have no doubt I shall be able to go with you to this ball. Hobbling is thought very becoming now-a-days. You have not told me why you are so anxious to see this gentleman. Who is he?"

"He is an Austrian," replied she; "yet, I understand, of a very noble and honourable character."

"You amuse me with your distinctions, Ellen," said Frank, interrupting her; "an Austrian, *yet* an honourable man! Do you mean to imply that Austrian gentlemen are not usually honourable men?"

"Perhaps I was wrong," said Ellen. "One is so apt to judge of individuals by their national character."

"Oh, that's it!" exclaimed Frank; "now I can agree with you; and I am perfectly willing to admit that an individual Austrian *may* be an honourable man, though nationally a sneak and coward of the most neutral-tinted dye. Well, and what about this gentleman?"

"He has been among the Russians in the Crimea," replied Ellen; "and I hope to obtain some information from him respecting the English prisoners. I have a sort of feverish hope that Reginald may be a prisoner."

Frank made no reply. He could not for a moment entertain the same hope, for had he not seen his friend's corpse consigned to the grave? But he would not needlessly dispel the flattering illusion to which she clung so desperately.

Ellen saw the feeling that caused his silence, and her eyes filled with tears. To hide the rising emotion she started up, and sought out Lady Willoughby, to announce her intention of accepting Miss Brownlow's invitation. Her ladyship had herself stood too much upon points of etiquette for her to make any objections to this arrangement; so she contented herself with patting the young lady's cheek, and calling her a dear little prude.

Ellen despatched a note to Miss Brownlow, and the same evening saw her established under that lady's protection, in a snug little house in Mayfair.

CHAPTER XIV.

THE FRIAR OF ORDERS GREY.

FRANK WILLOUGHBY was a daily visitor at Mayfair, much to his mother's satisfaction, who supposed that the whole of the time he spent with Ellen was employed in making progress in his matrimonial speculation.

Miss Brownlow, being a woman of a very different stamp, was taken into the young people's confidence; and having a Banshee in her own family, was much impressed by Ellen's account of the Death Wail of the Hawkshawes, and fully agreed with her in believing that the last descendant of the original stock would not die without the usual warning.

If Ellen had felt comforted by Oliver's expressions of faith, how much more consolation and support did she derive from the concurrence of a woman of sense and education, like Miss Brownlow!

The evening of Mrs. Livingstone's party, where Ellen hoped to meet the Austrian, at length arrived. Frank had promised his assistance, as he could ask more direct questions than she could put with propriety.

The rooms were crowded, but the Austrian had not arrived. Frank strove to enliven his companion's drooping spirits, and Miss Brownlow whispered words of comfort in her other ear.

"I trust I shall not be so foolish as to faint," said Ellen; "let me sit in this quiet corner for a few moments, and then, my dear friend, I will ask you to take me home."

"I will fetch you a glass of wine," said

Frank, and away he limped, looking very interesting in his uniform, with his pale face and slender figure.

"There are some fresh arrivals," said Miss Brownlow, "but I heard no Austrian name. However, if you think you can be left with safety, I will just go and see who they are."

"Pray do," said Ellen, eagerly; "I can be left quite safely, and I will not stir till you return."

Ellen sat in the dreary solitude of the crowd. Immediately after Miss Brownlow's departure she became aware that the fresh arrivals were a party from a *bal costumé*, who were expected to show themselves, and pass an hour or two. The music struck up again; dancing was renewed with redoubled animation; and the whole scene swam before her like a troubled dream, over which chronology brooded like a nightmare.

Charles the Second whirled past, whispering characteristic gallantries to a young damsel in the costume of the nineteenth century. Henry the Eighth was polking with Miss Brown; while Mary Queen of Scots, some three hundred years after her execution, skipped lightly, and flirted while she skipped, with Captain Dashwood of the Hussars. Then there were plenty of Turks talking perfectly vernacular English; and one or two young Turkish ladies, who suffered their unveiled faces to be gazed on by crowds of infidels, fearless of the bowstring, the sack, and the Bosphorus.

Ellen's eyes were fixed anxiously on the spot where Frank had disappeared. A weight which she could scarcely endure oppressed her spirits, and she watched for his return, to conduct her to Miss Brownlow's carriage. She could sit there, she thought, in the cool air of the street, and if she did faint, there would be no one to see her.

A deep sigh fell on her ear. She turned, and saw standing beside her a tall figure, which she immediately recognised as one of the maskers, habited as a " Friar of Orders Grey." His cowl was drawn over the upper part of his face, and from beneath it hung a long white beard.

As he drew nearer to her, she observed that his movements were slow and faltering, and that he leaned heavily on his staff for support.

" Have I been rightly informed, young lady," he said, in a deep sepulchral tone, " that you are Miss Maynard?"

" That is my name," she replied, hardly able to repress the agitation that she felt.

" *Ellen* Maynard?" repeated the stranger, interrogatively.

" Yes—yes!" she responded, hurriedly.

" Then I have a message to deliver to you, from one who fell in the East," said the stranger. " May I be permitted to sit beside you?"

Ellen tried to gasp out her consent, but could only indicate it with her hand.

"I must apologise for not raising my hood," said the stranger, sitting near enough to be heard without difficulty, but not so near as to appear obtrusive. "I too have been a soldier, and have a wound on my face, which renders me for the present unpresentable to ladies' eyes."

"Make no excuses, sir," said Ellen, "but tell me, I entreat of you, what was the message?"

"Do you not ask who sent it?" inquired the stranger.

"I know—I know too well!" replied Ellen. "It could be but *one*."

"The name of him who gave me this message was Reginald Hawkshawe," said the stranger.

"*Was!*" repeated Ellen, clasping her hands in agony, "oh, do not say *was!* It *is* his name, for I am sure he is not—cannot—*must* not be dead!"

"I was present when he fell," said the friar. "His last words were a prayer for your happiness, and the message which he desired me to deliver to you, if ever I had the opportunity, was to ask you to pray for him sometimes at the grave on the sea-beach; to think of him with as much kindness as you can; and to take care of his horse and dog, the only living creatures that love him. Also," and here the friar's voice had a hard and constrained tone in it—"he desires that you will speedily marry the man you love; and may you be happy with him!"

The stranger rose and turned to go, but Ellen's broken words detained him.

"The man I love is dead!" she exclaimed, starting to her feet. "Frank Willoughby is as a brother to me. I love Reginald Hawkshawe! But he is dead, you say,

and I will have no other husband. Oh,
Reginald! Reginald! Reginald!"

The words seemed wrenched with agony
from her bosom. She spread out her arms
as if seeking support, and fell forward on
the floor.

Frank and Miss Brownlow were close at
hand, and they raised her before her fall
had attracted much notice. Neither of
them had particularly remarked the friar,
who mixed with the crowd on their appearance. A side door was near, and through
this Frank managed to convey the senseless
girl, notwithstanding his lameness. The
cool air revived her, and she crawled down
to the carriage, without making any com-
motion among the visitors.

Miss Brownlow herself superintended the
operation of putting her to bed, and left
her apparently asleep. But Ellen's grief
required to withdraw itself from every eye,
even the kindest and most sympathetic, and

the night was passed in tears and wakefulness.

Miss Brownlow's maid entered her mistress's room rather earlier than usual, and in answer to the lady's inquiry after Miss Maynard's health, presented to her a note, saying she supposed Miss Maynard was better, as she was able to take a journey.

"A journey!" said Miss Brownlow. "What do you mean? Where is she gone?"

"I don't know, ma'am," replied the servant; "only she set off about eight o'clock this morning, and told Susan to let you have this note as soon as you were awake."

"Draw back the curtains, Goodwin," said Miss Brownlow. "I want to know what is amiss."

The note was as follows:—

"You know all the feelings of my heart,

16—2

my dear friend,—all my hopes, and all my sorrows; and therefore I need not apologise for my abrupt departure, further than by explaining the cause of it. Last night I spoke with one who saw *him* fall, and received his last words, and a message to me. I have no doubt now—no hope. I shall depart in half an hour for St. Osyth's, for I cannot endure even a look of sympathy at present. Among the scenes that are endeared to me by —— [The page was here rendered illegible by the tears that had fallen upon it.] I cannot write more now. In a few days you shall hear from me again.   Yours affectionately,

"ELLEN MAYNARD."

By the time this note was read there were fresh tears upon it, and then the warm-hearted old lady (she was an Irishwoman) lay down and sobbed for an hour. Perhaps some early recollections were

aroused by Ellen's sorrows; perhaps it was
only the warm impulsive Hibernian blood,
and glowing imagination that so readily
made another's woes her own.

Goodwin was just ascending the stairs
with a cup of tea for her mistress, when a
thundering double knock at the street door
caused her to stop and listen. There was
something remarkable in the knock. It
was not the performance of a footman; it
was some impetuous gentleman, in a violent
hurry.

Such a knock was sure to be answered
promptly, and in a moment she heard
Frank Willoughby's voice, asking for Miss
Maynard. A dialogue ensued between the
impatient young soldier and the porter, in
which the humble tones of the latter being
lost in a confused murmur, only the speeches
of the former were distinguishable; but
from them Goodwin could gather the sense
of the whole.

" Gone!—gone where?"—A murmur.

"What the deuce! Eight o'clock this morning! And left no message?"—Murmur.

" Is Miss Brownlow up yet?"—Murmur.

" Never mind! I *must* see her! It's an affair of life and death, and a great deal more besides. Where's her maid?"

Another murmur, followed by a bounding and hopping up the stairs, accompanied by muttered imprecations upon his lame leg, and Frank stood beside the lady's maid, outside Miss Brownlow's chamber door.

"So your mistress is not up yet, Goodwin?" he asked.

" No, sir," replied the servant.

" Tell her I want to speak to her on a most important subject," said Frank. " I'll keep my eyes shut, or be blindfolded, if she will only admit me for just two minutes."

" Goodwin! who is there?" called the lady from within.

" It's Captain Willoughby, ma'am, wanting particularly to speak to you."

" Has anything dreadful happened?" cried Miss Brownlow, quite forgetting, in her anxiety about Ellen, to consider whether her nightcap was becomingly arranged. " Oh, Frank, make haste and tell me what it is! Has she done anything rash?"

" It seems rather rash to bolt so suddenly," said Frank, advancing into the room; " but what I want to know is where she is gone?"

" Read that note," said Miss Brownlow. " That's all I know about it."

Frank read it, sitting on the edge of the old lady's bed. Then he whispered a few words to her, that Goodwin might not hear what he said. A short colloquy followed in the same cautious tones, and Frank took his leave, descending the staircase with wonderful rapidity by a means which I am sorry to have to record of an officer in Her Majesty's army—namely, sliding down the balusters.

The moment Frank was gone Miss Brownlow jumped up, and dressed in a great hurry. During the whole of the day she bustled and fidgeted about, and seemed to be expecting somebody to come, or something to happen; yet no one unusual called upon her, and nothing particular occurred. She went to bed with great deliberation, as though she might receive a summons at any stage of the proceedings; and the following morning she got up early in a hurry, and was in a hurry till the afternoon, when she received a telegraphic message, at which she laughed immoderately, at intervals, for the rest of the day. And yet there seemed nothing very witty or humorous in the · message, for it contained only these words—" Frank Willoughby to Miss Brownlow. All's serene."

CHAPTER XV.

AT an early hour on the same day that Miss
Brownlow received the telegraphic message
from Frank Willoughby, the unhappy
mistress of St. Osyth's Priory wandered
through the garden, now her own property.

She had arrived late on the previous
night, and had lain awake till the dawn.
The few servants who remained, had
welcomed her with tears.   Hector alone
seemed joyful, and even he, after his first
salutation, looked wistfully in her face, and
whined, and asked as plainly as dog could
ask, where was his master?

As Ellen wandered about the well-known garden paths, the faithful animal followed her with drooping head, sympathising with her grief.

"Hector," she said, in a plaintive voice, "where is your master?"

The dog seemed to understand her, and whined piteously.

"I have not seen Ganymede yet, Hector," she continued, as though the creature could comprehend her words. "He shall come out here with us. He misses his master too."

She went into the library and rang the bell. Oliver obeyed the summons.

"Tell the groom to bring Mr. Reginald's horse, Ganymede, round into the garden;" said Ellen.

"Yes, Miss," replied the old man, astonished at the unusual order, but too respectful to express anything beyond implicit obedience. "If you please, Miss, here is a small parcel that Master Reginald left with me for you. It's your keys, I think."

"Thank you, Oliver," she said, taking the packet with a trembling hand.

"If you please, Miss," he continued, with great diffidence and hesitation, "will you forgive me for making so bold, but do you really think there is no hope? We have not heard any sounds yet."

"I have spoken to a gentleman who was with him when he fell," she replied, bursting into tears. "No, Oliver! there is no hope—none! Except the hope that I may soon follow him, and end a life that is too miserable to be borne!"

"Don't take on so, Miss!" cried the old man, while the tears flowed down his withered cheeks; "dear Miss! pray don't! Seek for comfort from One above. You have often found comfort there before; and you know that those who seek faithfully never seek in vain."

" Presently I shall be able to do so," said the young lady, " but now I could only pray for death. He sent me a message, Oliver, asking me to be kind to his horse and dog. So send Ganymede round to the garden. Those poor dumb creatures are the only companions I can endure now."

She returned to the garden, and if she had been able to take any heed of time, she would have found that her orders were not obeyed very promptly. But she sat on the grass beside the stream, watching the sparkling eddies with a vacant eye, in that stagnant condition of mind, which only those who have suffered deep and hopeless sorrow can fully comprehend, and which makes them feel, when aroused from it, how blessed a thing insanity or death must be.

The delay was caused by Oliver's having heard a ring at the outer gate, as he passed by to take the message to the stables, and his stopping to answer it.

A post-chaise was outside, and a young, military-looking man, with bright blue eyes and chestnut hair, stood at the wicket.

" Is Miss Maynard here?" he demanded, impatiently.

" Yes, sir," replied the old servant.

" Is she well?" was the next inquiry.

A head, much muffled in a travelling cloak and cap, was bent forward in the chaise, as if to catch the replies.

"She's not exactly ill, sir," said Oliver, "but I can't say she is well. I am sure she can't see any visitors, sir."

" We'll see about that," was the half-laughing reply. " Your name is Oliver, is it not?"

" Yes, sir," said Oliver, just preparing to draw back and shut the wicket, for he began to suspect an invasion from the heir-at-law.

" Just come to the chaise-door, then, will you, to speak to this gentleman," said the military-looking man who had hitherto addressed him.

"Thank you, sir," replied the cautious old servant, "but perhaps the gentleman will have the kindness to state his business before I leave my mistress's gate un-guarded."

The head in the chaise bent forward again, the cap was off, and the collar of the cloak pulled down.

"Oliver!" said the voice belonging to the head; and the old man sprang forward with the activity of youth, and clung trembling to the chaise door.

"Oh, come! I say—I say," cried the young military man, supporting Oliver by the arm lest he should fall. "Keep up, man! Why, this is too much for him!"

The postillions were twisting themselves round in their saddles, trying to see what was going on; but all they could make out was that the military gentleman opened the chaise door, and pushed Oliver in, but stood outside himself while the three held a conference in subdued, but cheerful tones. Oliver then jumped out, with a " Yes, sir! yes, sir! It shall be done directly!" and ran back into the courtyard, leaving the wicket open behind him.

The postillions were then paid and dismissed, somewhat dissatisfied at not having been able to unravel the mystery.

The garden was too remote from the entrance-hall for Ellen to hear the sound of the wheels, and if it had reached her, it would have fallen upon unheeding ears, as she sat, mechanically caressing Hector's soft ears with one hand, and with the other plucking blades of grass and setting them to float on the stream. For the time she was in a state of harmless and unrepulsive idiotcy.

At the sound of a horse's hoofs on the gravelled path she started as from a sleep, and stared round her.

"Shall I bring him on to the grass, Miss?" asked the groom who was leading Ganymede. "I'm afeard he'll cut up the turf sadly."

"I do not care for the turf. Bring him here," she replied, and took the bridle from him. "Thank you, John. That will do. You can go now. I will send for you when I want you to take him back."

The groom looked dubious; scratched his head, shook it slowly, and then retreated; for there was a dignity in Ellen's grief that commanded implicit obedience.

She stood with the bridle in her hand, watching the man's departure, before she ventured to give utterance to her emotions. When the clang of the gate told her it was closed, she threw her arms round the neck of the noble animal, and talked to him in broken accents of his lost master. The horse looked at her with his large, full eyes, and whinnied softly, and seemed as much depressed as Hector had been.

Yes,—as Hector *had* been; for what ailed the dog now? With one paw resting against Ganymede's flank, he stood on his hinder legs, and sniffed at the horse's shoulder, uttering a succession of eager whines, broken by an occasional sharp bark, as though he were on the scent of some quarry.

When in the chaise, Oliver had kissed and pressed *a hand*. He had afterwards patted Ganymede's shoulder in the stable. Did the keen scent inherited from his blood-hound ancestors enable Hector to detect the faint trace thus conveyed?

"You think your dear master is coming now to mount Ganymede," said poor Ellen, addressing the dog; "but he will never come again, Hector! never—never—never come again!"

Her four-footed friends seemed to have

lost all sympathy for her; for Ganymede,
now looking over her shoulder towards the
library windows, in which he perhaps saw
his own image reflected, arched his neck,
pricked his small ears, and neighed long
and joyously.

"He will not come for thy calling, poor
Ganymede," said Ellen, caressing his neck.
But now the dog began again, and his
demonstrations were so singular that they
attracted her attention. He was crouching
on the ground, trembling till every hair
seemed to quiver distinctly, and dragging
himself towards some object behind her,
uttering all the while the most piteous
sounds. The horse neighed again, and
stretched his yearning neck over her
shoulder.

Ellen turned, and there, close behind her,
stood the figure she had seen at the ball,—
the "Friar of Orders Grey."

The cowl was still drawn over his face.

17—2

He no longer, however, leaned feebly on his staff, but stood, with folded arms, drawn up to his full majestic height. Another change she also noticed—the white beard was gone, and in its place a thick black one was plainly visible.

It was now Ellen's turn to tremble. She stood fixed, gazing at the figure. Still it moved not. She rubbed her eyes; but it did not vanish. And the dog was now at his feet, licking them; but he did not notice him. The horse, released from her gentle hold, approached him, and whinnied a soft recognition; but he did not move. At length the arms unfolded themselves. He took one step forward and extended them. Ellen shrieked out the name of Reginald, and sprang into the friar's embrace.

"My darling! my own darling!" murmured a deep well-known voice, as the cowl bent down and covered her face also. Then from beneath it proceeded a most unfriar-like sound; for the friar was certainly kissing her, and she as certainly made no resistance, though I should be sorry to say she kissed him in return. "My dearest one! my own Ellen!" he murmured again.

"How could you be so cruel as to tell me you were dead?" she whispered.

"I could not suppose it would grieve you, dearest," he replied. "I had heard that you still went into company after the report of my death had reached you, so I could not think you mourned for my loss."

"It was because I hoped you were still living, and I wanted to hear news of you," said Ellen.

"Yes, Frank Willoughby has told me all about that," said Reginald. "The only person who knew I was alive was one of the party of masqueraders who went that night to Mrs. Livingstone's. He ascertained that you were to be there, and introduced me in this disguise; for I longed to see you

again, and perhaps to hear you speak before
I set off for the backwoods of America,
where I meant to hide myself. The first
person I recognised was Frank; and you
were leaning on his arm. It was only
what I expected, but my heart was torn
with grief and jealousy. I felt that I
could not endure it any longer, and was
just going away, to start by the night
train for Liverpool, when I turned for one
last look, and saw that he had left you.
An irresistible feeling led me back. There
was an elderly lady with you, but she too
went away. You know the rest. Your
first eager words startled me; but it was
not till the last, when you fell on the floor,
that I could believe that you really loved
me. But that crowded ball-room was no
place for explanations. Already there were
curious eyes upon us, and as I saw Frank
and your old lady-friend at hand to assist
you, I made my escape. I waited in the

street, expecting to see you come out; but all in vain. I did not of course know where to find you, so about the time when you were flying down here by the railway, I was rousing up Frank Willoughby, whom I easily found, and asking him for an explanation. What he told me made all clear; and he sprang up as if the drums were beating to arms, and went off to break the intelligence to you. He found your old friend crying her eyes out over your note; but left her in a very different mood. We came down together, and here we are!" he exclaimed. At which period a repetition of the uncanonical sounds occurred.

"Oh! Reginald!" said Ellen, "is it really Reginald? I can't believe it is true! Yet this is my Reginald's black beard, and the horse and dog know you. But why do you keep this hood over your face? Are you really wounded?"

"Not very severely," he replied, throwing

back the cowl, and showing a strip of black plaster on his temple. "It is rather ornamental than otherwise. Don't you think so?"

"How did you get it?" she inquired. "And how did you get back? I want to know everything."

"How impatient we have become all at once!" said Reginald; "I got it in the skirmish wherein I was supposed to be killed. I lay senseless for some time, but was discovered by a Russian officer to whom I had rendered a service some months before."

"I know—I know!" cried Ellen, eagerly, "that officer with a young wife, whom you carried to his own men, and——"

"Ay, ay, that very one, fortunately," interrupted Reginald; "I see Frank has told you all my exploits. With the help of a soldier whom he could trust, he took off my uniform, and dressed me in the clothes of a huge Russian, whose body I understood was afterwards buried for mine. I was then taken off to the hospital, and through his interest, treated with great care. He came frequently to see me, but we could not talk much, as my cue was to appear half insensible that I might not be obliged to speak, and so betray that I was an Englishman. As soon as I could be removed, he had me taken to his own house in Sebastopol, and after a few weeks he intrusted me to an Austrian gentleman, whom I accompanied through Russia as a fellow-countryman, my friend having obtained a passport for me under an Austrian name. Then I found the advantage of the German you had taught me, for it suddenly became my native tongue, and I could speak nothing else."

"And this Austrian must have been the very gentleman I went to that ball purposely to see!" said Ellen.

"The very same," replied Reginald; "Frank and I have had it all over, for you may imagine we could not sleep on our way from town."

"And you are really Reginald?" she said, looking into his face with an expression of blended joy and doubt, "I can hardly believe it! I think it must be a dream!"

"What's your opinion, Hector? What do you say to it, Ganymede? Am I myself, or merely a dream of Miss Ellen's?" he asked, addressing his two fourfooted favourites.

The creatures, who had evidently felt themselves unduly neglected, testified unbounded joy at his words, and the caresses that accompanied them. Hector jumped and barked, and Ganymede, after laying his head on his master's shoulder and shouting a most inspiriting neigh into his ear, took advantage of his freedom to kick up his heels and scamper off round the garden, followed by his canine friend, who doubtless thought it was his duty to take care of him.

Had there been any eyes at liberty to look into the library while this scene was passing in the garden, they might have beheld a performance much resembling that of Ganymede;—namely, a pair of legs kicking up in the air in a most wonderful manner. The owner of them was Frank · Willoughby.

When Reginald first went into the garden Frank stood breathlessly watching his proceedings.

When Ellen sprang into his arms, Frank repressed the shout of delight that struggled for utterance, and falling back on the sofa, demonstrated his satisfaction in the gymnastic fashion above-mentioned. Then came a fear lest the sudden joy had been too much for her, and he looked out. All went right, and he fell down and kicked again, and went on alternately looking and kicking, till roused by a double peal of laughter, when he found Reginald and Ellen standing in the room.

"Oh, but I say, isn't this jolly!" he exclaimed, wringing both their hands. "By-the-bye, I must send a telegraphic message to that jolly old brick, Miss Brownlow. I promised I would."

And forthwith he penned that extremely concise message which we have already seen, and dispatched it by the groom.

"There is one point that we have quite overlooked, Willoughby," said Reginald, when the young man came back into the library. "I stand at present somewhat in the position of a deserter. I must return to London without loss of time, and report myself."

"Of course you must," said Frank, looking serious for a moment. "But you may rest this one night, I think, without any blame, especially as you are far from right yet, you know."

"Have you any other wound besides that on your forehead?" asked Ellen, anxiously.

"Yes, love, a sabre wound on my side, which still sometimes——" and he looked inside his coat; then, with a significant glance at Frank, he added, "Humph!"

"At it again?" inquired Frank. Reginald nodded.

"Oh! what is it?" cried Ellen. "What is amiss? Does it bleed?"

"Sometimes," replied Reginald; "but nothing to be alarmed about. Go out of the room, dear, and Frank can manage to bind it up."

"If you cannot do it, call me, for I can," whispered Ellen to Frank, as she hurried out.

In a few minutes she heard her name shouted aloud by Frank, and running in, found Reginald with his coat off, lying on the sofa, almost insensible; his right side was partially uncovered, disclosing a ghastly wound from which the blood was streaming.

"I cannot stop it," cried Frank, who was quite unnerved and trembling; "and he will bleed to death!"

Ellen had never seen such a spectacle; but with that truly womanly courage and presence of mind which seem only to exist in such emergencies, she commenced her operations.

"Ring for a sponge and water, and some brandy," she said, holding the sides of the wound together; "and put his arm down by his side—for its present attitude draws the wound open."

Poor Frank had raised the arm, not thinking of the effect it would have. He placed it as she directed, and ran off to fetch what she wanted. At the door he met Oliver, who was just coming in with a card.

"Fetch some brandy, and a sponge and

basin of water," exclaimed Frank, mechanically glancing at the card. "Hurrah!
we're all right," he added. "Ellen! here's
Smedley come, in the nick of time!"

Out he rushed, and returned immediately,
dragging in the doctor.

Reginald tried to raise his eyes, and
smiling faintly, held out his hand to Ellen's
old friend.

"Keep quiet, will you!" said the doctor,
snappishly. "That's right, my dear. Hold
it just so. Sponge and water!—That's
right," he said, to Oliver, who had just
brought them in. "Now some brandy!"

"Sit down, Oliver," said Frank, putting
the old servant into a chair, for he was
quite overcome by the sight of his master
bleeding to death, as he thought—"I'll
fetch the brandy."

"Here's the key, sir," he replied. "One
of the maids will show you where it is
kept."

Frank hopped away with great activity, and Oliver tried to rise.

"Sit still—sit still, old friend," said Ellen, turning her pale face towards him, with one of her sweet smiles.

Reginald put his hand caressingly on her head.

"Can't you keep quiet?" exclaimed Mr. Smedley, sharply, as he put the hand back again. "You must not stir."

The doctor snapped at everybody except Ellen, until the wound was bound up, and the patient made comfortable.

"Now," said he, "my dear girl, go and wash your hands."

"Presently," she replied; "but I want to see how he gets on, first."

"Wash it off, Ellen!" whispered Reginald, in a very faint voice, but with a mischievous smile, "it is so *dirty !*"

"I do not think so," said Ellen, blushing.

"Come nearer—I want to whisper to

you," said he; and she leaned over him—
"the handkerchief is still over my heart.
Is it *dirty* to wear it there?"

"No," she murmured, softly.

"Are your crimsoned hands disgusting to
you?" he asked. "Do you turn sick at the
sight of them?"

"I was sick at the thought that you
might die," replied Ellen; "but the blood
itself is dear to me. *Your* blood cannot be
disgusting."

"Ah! then you have learned your lesson.
Ellen! *now* you love! Do you remember
what I said when I was a wild, untutored
savage? Savage as I was, though, love had
made me wiser than you on one point."

"I cannot allow so much talking," said
Mr. Smedley, interrupting the whispered
conversation of the lovers. "Miss Ellen!
Obey orders, and wash your hands. In a
few days he will be able to talk enough to
satisfy even feminine curiosity."

"Will you stay with him, sir?" asked Ellen.

"Certainly I will, as long as it is necessary," replied Mr. Smedley; "and with such a doctor and such a nurse he cannot fail to get well."

"But I," said Ellen, dubiously, "I must not stay, I fear."

"Do you want to kill me?" cried Reginald, with one of his old fierce looks, as he raised himself on the sofa.

"Hush!—hush!—keep quiet!" said the doctor, trying to put him down again, but the sudden excitement had given Reginald so much strength, that he found it impossible to do so. "Don't agitate yourself. She shall not go."

"It is not her going or staying that I care for," he said, trembling with emotion; "it is her cruelty in wishing to go."

"I do not wish to go, dearest Reginald!" cried Ellen, in tears, "I only thought I ought not to stay."

"If you think you ought to go, pray do so," said Reginald, falling back on the pillows.

"I will not go, indeed I will not!" exclaimed Ellen, terrified at his paleness, and the doctor's uneasy glance.

"Will you be married by special licence in a day or two?" asked Reginald, in a weak voice.

"Yes—yes—anything you wish," she replied.

He pressed her hand, but turned so pale that Mr. Smedley administered a little more brandy.

"Don't look so frightened, you little fool!" said Reginald, as the faintness passed away. "I am not going to die yet, for I have something to live for. But I am sure the doctor will tell you that you must not vex me, nor contradict me in anything."

"Indeed you must not," responded Mr.

18 –2

Smedley; "you have had sufficient proof of that, I think."

"You need not caution me to be careful," said Ellen, "I will not oppose him in anything again."

"You are a witness to her promise, doctor," said Reginald, smiling.

Ellen thought of the promise she had given in her terror, to be married in a few days, and went off hastily to wash her hands.

CHAPTER XVI.

LAST SCENE OF ALL.

WHEN Ellen stood in the solitude of her chamber she could not but reflect on the change that had come over her whole existence since she had crept out of it in the morning, a broken-hearted, despairing creature, without a hope on this side the grave. Then her memory went back to the time when she had fled from it, on the fatal night of the fire. Again she beheld the old hag bending over her demoniacal work;—the wild music rang in her ears, and the face that imagination had pictured, gleamed pale and spirit-like through the window;—again she descended the slippery path, and was poised upon the sea in her frail bark—

> To cry to the waves that roar'd to her,
> To sigh to the winds, whose pity, sighing back again,
> Did her but loving wrong.

And again the red glare of the fire lighted up rock and wave.

Then came intervals of unconsciousness; a sense of hunger, and a burning thirst; some fleeting thoughts of Reginald, but the abiding feeling still was that of trust in heaven, and prayer for aid to bear meekly the trials that were allotted to her. Then followed the sudden plunge into the water, and, heard amid all the din, the loud barking of a dog. All after was dark as the tomb, till she found herself at Mrs. Franklyn's.

The subsequent events passed in equally rapid review before her; every incident as distinct as when it happened. Probably

her memory was strengthened by this
exercise, for she suddenly recollected, with
perfect clearness, the whole of the gipsy's
dying prophecy.

"'They stand at the altar!'" she repeated. "It is to be so, then! How little
could I at that time imagine that those she
spoke of were Reginald and myself! And,
above all, that I should rejoice at it! And
he has my promise to marry him in a few
days! And Mr. Smedley says I must not
thwart him! How foolish I was to promise
so hastily! And yet—why should I regret
it? It will give me a right to nurse him,
—and what has he not done and suffered
for my sake! No—I must not thwart him!"

She fell into a reverie, from which she
at length started with the exclamation,
"Oh, how happy I am!" The still small
voice of conscience demanded if she was
also grateful. She had called unceasingly
upon her Saviour in the time of tribulation,

but had she recollected him in the hour of joy?

With an humbled heart she knelt and breathed her grateful thanks to Him who had watched over her through all her trials and dangers; and when she arose, the hurricane of joy had passed, and a calm and holy sense of happiness remained.

"Doctor," said Reginald, soon after Ellen had left the library, "when a dose of medicine has to be swallowed, don't you advise your patients to swallow it quickly, without stopping to think about it?"

"Certainly," replied Mr. Smedley; "but I have not prescribed any for you."

"I know that," said Reginald; "but I want you to impress the principle upon Ellen. She will, sooner or later, be obliged to swallow the bitter pill of swearing to obey; and I am of opinion that the sooner she gets it over, the better. Besides, she has scruples about propriety, and I don't

like to make her act against her opinion of
what is right, nor can I think of letting her
out of my sight again. All would be made
straight by a quiet marriage. She gave
her consent to it just now, in her fright,
and I shall keep her to her word. Your
advice will go a great way with her."

"It's rather sudden," said the old gentleman; "but, considering all the circumstances, I think it would be advisable."

"That's right," said Reginald. "Now
make her think so too."

"If Ellen has given her word," said
Frank, "she will not draw back from it.
I never knew her break a promise since she
was old enough to give one."

"Ah, Frank!" said Reginald, with a sigh,
"how many pleasant recollections you must
have, as the companion of Ellen's childhood! I never envied anyone before."

"And you'd better not begin now, old
fellow," replied Frank, laughing; "for with

all these pleasant recollections you might be obliged to take the extra-pleasant conscious-ness that your early intimacy had ensured for you her most *sisterly* affection."

"Keep your own associations, Frank, and keep the sisterly affection you have got," said Reginald; "my envious fit is over."

" I don't know whether mine is, though," said Frank to himself, pulling a long face as he looked out into the garden. "By-the-bye, Mr. Smedley," he continued, turn-ing round, after a few minute's contempla-tion, with his usual beaming expression of countenance, "we have not yet heard to what happy circumstance we owe your very opportune arrival here. You must think we live in a land of miracles, and that such an event as an angel suddenly popping down upon us, and sending in his card, is not a matter to cause us any astonishment."

" Your visit is so opportune," observed

Reginald, "that it seems ungrateful to ask why you came. Yet I must own to a share in Frank's curiosity."

"I had to go to town on business," said the doctor, "and heard from Captain Willoughby's lady mother that Miss Maynard had suddenly eloped by herself to St. Osyth's, and that the next train had taken down her dearly beloved son, and his friend Captain Hawkshawe, whom everybody had supposed to be dead. From various trifling details I gathered that the young lady, previous to her departure, was not aware of Captain Hawkshawe's return, and therefore, as I feared the too sudden joy might throw her into a brain fever, I followed. So there is the explanation of the whole mystery."

Ellen soon after re-entered, and they spent a happy evening together.

The next morning Mr. Smedley, in accordance with his promise to Reginald, sounded Ellen respecting the advisability of a speedy marriage.

"I see he has asked you to persuade me," she said; "but that is needless. I have already given him my word."

Reginald was enchanted, but consented to extend his few days to a fortnight, by which time he was able to go to the parish church, which Ellen very much preferred to a marriage by special licence in the library, which, she said, would not be like being married at all.

The wedding was so quiet, that not even the villagers were aware of it till it was over, and then the bells rang merrily all the rest of the day, and old and young feasted on a banquet that had been privately prepared by Reginald's order at the Priory, under the superintendence of Mrs. Sweetman, who had returned to her former, and more congenial duties.

Mrs. Hawkshawe was considerably improved in health and intellect. She recollected but little of the sorrows that had preceded her insanity; but as the Priory seemed to arouse painful feelings, Reginald made an arrangement, advantageous to both parties, for her to reside with Mr. and Mrs. Franklyn, with whom she lives, as happy and harmless as a child. Reginald and his gentle wife visit them frequently.

Oliver has finally quitted service, and now holds the office of parish clerk, for which he is well fitted.

Lady Willoughby went into violent hysterics on hearing of Ellen's marriage with Reginald, but as Mr. Smedley was not at hand she was compelled to " come to " by herself.

During a subsequent interview with her ladyship, the doctor hinted at some meditated disposition of his own property, which might affect Frank's future prospects, and was only warned by a little premature tenderness on the part of the deceased knight's relict, that she had interpreted his inuendoes into the preliminaries of a proposal of marriage to herself!

More alarmed than he had ever been at the most desperate case which had come into his hands during the course of a long professional career, the poor doctor all but lost his presence of mind. However, he managed to undeceive her, without letting her see that he was aware of the error into which she had fallen, his intention being simply to make Frank his heir.

Her ladyship immediately became less sentimental, but far more rational than he had ever supposed her capable of being.

Frank is steadier than he used to be, and keeps his promise to Reginald and Mr. Smedley never to touch cards or dice, nor bet upon a horse.

And now I ought, in old-fashioned style, to say that Reginald and Ellen lived happily all the rest of their lives; but it will be more in accordance with actual experience to say, that there seems every probability of their continuing through life, as happy as they are at the period at which my story closes.

THE END.

LONDON:
SAVILL AND EDWARDS, PRINTERS,
CHANDOS-STREET.